JEWELS OF EYES
by Dian Scott

This book is a work of fiction. Names, characters, places, and incidents either are products of the author's imagination or are used fictitiously. Any resemblance to actual events or locales or persons, living or dead, is entirely coincidental.

ISBN: 978-1-62660-137-6

Book design by Michael Campbell at MCWriting.com

Jewels of Eyes

DIAN SCOTT

To my husband

CONTENTS

Chapter 1

T HE MEET AND GREET party was a political function
for a politician representing the state of New York. It was
being hosted by his very well to do friends helping to
promote his political agenda. The host' home was huge, with
dark mahogany wood, and a spiraling staircase with windows
that followed the curve of the stairs, appearing as though it
went up into the sky. Layered insets in the ceilings, and crown
molding trim setting off every room. The halls, the doorways,
furnishings, everything was massive and heavy. No doubt
money abounded. Buffet tables were set up with colorful food
while wait staff was making sure every guest had plenty to
drink. Having plenty to drink would later help the prominent
attendees open their wallets and checkbooks to financially
support the candidate of choice.

The small boy stood in the crowd of people towering over
him, feeling timid, yet mischievous. He knew his mother had
directed him to be on his best behavior and he was trying.
What was there for such a small boy to do at these stuffy
adult events? The boy's father always had a kind word or a
quick wink of the eye when his mother wasn't looking, but
most of the time he was gone, always traveling with his work.
The child found himself alone with his mother, and even she
left him in the care of house staff or his current nanny most
of the time.

Little Timothy stood by the tables of food and watched as
people stuffed their faces with elaborate canapés and gave fake
laughs at the endless chatter of some of the more prominent

adults. He picked at the finely cut vegetables on one table, stuck his fingers in the jello molds at another, and considered what else he could do without getting caught. Suddenly, in his own childlike way, he thought he had the cleverest idea ever. Discreetly he crawled under one of buffet tables and waited for his first bit of entertainment.

As the first pair of wingtip shoes came up under the edge of the drape of the buffet table, the boy hurriedly tied the shoes together and he then turned and quickly, but softly touched the legs of the woman standing on the backside of the table. The woman yelped in surprise, causing the man with the wingtips to jump and then stumble, losing his balance and falling backwards, while his shoe laces snapped apart. Food and drink went flying, showering several of the guests.

While everyone rushed to help the fallen man, the woman on the backside of the table quickly leaned over, raised the drape on the table, and discovered the little boy sitting there with his hand over his mouth trying to smother his laughter. The woman hollered at the child to come out of there, and he did, petrified by the tone of her voice. The woman was the child's own mother, and the gentleman who fell backwards after her yelp, was the Ambassador of Royal Services of England.

The red headed woman took the child by the hand and rounded the table to the Ambassador and with a shake of the child's arm she said, "Our beloved, but mischievous son has something to say to you, Ambassador." With that the small child looked into the glaring green eyes of his mother and then to the man and said, "I am so sorry, sir, I only wanted to have some fun." The Ambassador laughed slightly and said, "Well, I would guess it's past your bedtime by now, young chap. Goodnight now." With those words, the boy's mother marched him up to his room.

He spotted his father in the crowd as they went up the long winding stairs, but his father quickly looked away, as though he did not see, just as he always did when the boy's mother was about to discipline him. The boy prayed they would never reach the top of the stairs. Once alone in his room with his mother, he was subjected to repeated slaps in the face and each time he stood back up, she would grab him by the arms and pull him close to her face so she could keep her voice down. She would glare at him with her green eyes and threaten of what she would do to him if there were not people downstairs.

Finally, after expressing her total disgust with him and his behavior, she threw him in his clothes closet and turned the key in the lock. The child crouched in the corner of the dark closet. Then he pulled down the shirt he kept hung in the corner to comfort him each time she did this to him. He had spent far too many hours, even nights hunkering in this corner.

The shirt was one of his fathers. The housekeeper had thrown it out one day and little Timothy retrieved it. He had walked by the bag of clothes for the trash man, and had smelled his father's cologne. The shirt, with the scent of his father, had become his security blanket in the dark closet.

Timothy closed his eyes and recalled what his mother had said to him. She said she wasn't through, she would be back, how much more could she hurt him, he wondered? He hoped his father would intervene, although he never had, the little boy still hoped. His mother frightened him worse than any monster he had ever seen on television. He thought of how close she had gotten in his face. She was so angry her eyes had bulged while she scolded and threatened him. They were green like jewels, but tonight they had red all around them from her tears and anger. She said he had embarrassed her for the last time, the very last time. What exactly did that mean, he thought?

The eight year old drifted off into a fitful sleep, crouched in the corner of the dark closet. Visions of his mothers' angry bulging eyes in his mind, with only his father's old shirt to protect him for however long she chose to leave him locked up this time.

The tutors came and went; none stayed too long, for none could tolerate the domineering woman, Timothy's mother, for very long. The tutors never mentioned the bruises on the sides of the boy's head or the occasional busted lips. Once a female tutor had even ruffled the boy's hair in a joking manner. The child burst into tears and held his head. The tutor was scared of what she might have done to hurt him so, but when she looked closer while trying to comfort him, she found new lumps and bumps on top of old yellow bruises, as well as small clumps of hair missing.

The woman contemplated going to Child Welfare Services, but knew she could just as likely be deported, for all her paperwork to hold a job in this country was not in order. She watched closely and spent a great deal of time playing and teaching the little boy. The tutor knew all the while the mother was jealous of the companionship between herself and Timothy, and she knew her days working for this woman were probably numbered just for that reason.

It did not take long for the tutor's predictions to come to light, for suddenly, without warning, she was sent back to her native Costa Rica. The young tutor was hurt by the actions of the mother, but she did not realize the devastation and hurt it would bring to the small boy. For she was the only adult he had really gotten close to, shared and even laughed with.

The boy vowed then that one day his mother would not control his life and when that time came, he would never look back, he would never visit, or even talk to her again. He despised the woman who proclaimed to be his mother. For she was no mother, she was a living, breathing hell.

The following afternoon the closet doors were thrown open with the intense fury of a hurricane. Timothy, who had needed to go to the bathroom for the last few hours, in his dreaded fear, suddenly urinated all over himself. As his mother grabbed him by the hair and pulled him from his corner in the closet, she smelled the urine as it continued to run like an endless stream from the boy.

She swung at him with the leather shaving strap she kept hidden from her husband and the housekeepers. It was the same leather strap her father had used on her when she would not comply with his "secret wishes". She was beaten into submission. And now, after doing her "wifely duties", once married to the prominent young man handpicked by her parents, she had become pregnant and given birth to a male child. A male child that so reminded her of her father it made her crazy, for all she wanted to do was to torment and beat him the way she had been beaten.

Her husband was refused any attempts to get close to her after their son was born, she didn't want to have any more children, so after a while, he gave up trying. A man with his good looks and wealth should not have to beg from his own wife. He found soon afterward there were other women who would oblige him and tend to his needs. The gap between him and his wife grew ever greater. So great he failed to recognize his wife was taking her anger towards him and her hatred towards her father out on their only son.

The father was too busy playing corporate political games, building an empire for his son to one day take over. And when he wasn't in the corporate world he was busy satisfying his own selfish whims with women he had all over the country. His attitude towards his son was that he had no time for him now, he was busy building the child's future, let his mother and the endless number of nannies and tutors raise him. He felt when the time was right, he would step in and teach his son what he needed to know about life.

All he ever offered his son was a quick wink or a pat on the back. Each night in his prayers, which the little boy said silently after getting into bed because his mother did not believe in prayer; the boy would pray if there is a real God, please come and protect me. If you can't do that, then please make my father come and protect me, make him come and take me away from her. Please make my daddy save me from her, please. His daddy never saved him.

Like his mother, he began to believe there was no God, and the only one who could save him was himself. He knew he had to get away, but how, where would a little boy go? As the child ran from her leather strap he continually repeated to himself, "I hate her, I hate her."

The woman, in her mental sickness, beat the child mercilessly, all the while she called him names, the names she had longed to call her own father, names that were so demeaning the boy had no spirit left. He only had dreams. Dreams of getting far away and of getting even with his mother. His dreams would never fade, he would find a way to make them come true.

No one was aware of the dreadful chain that was being linked, no one could have predicted the impact these events would have on so many others' lives one day. The sins of some, the burdens of many. Like a thrown hand grenade, pain and suffering cast in an ever growing circle of victims, where does it all end?

Chapter 2

I T SEEMED LIKE she had been on the plane forever. She had looked at the back of the seat in front of her for seven hours now, gone to the restroom twice, and watched a movie that she had paid several dollars to see at the theater. She had tried to read a paperback novel, looked through some magazines, picked at the meal of grilled chicken and broccoli the flight attendant served, and listened to the woman seated beside her snore as she tried to doze a little herself.

Before leaving her home in Texas she had been eager to board the plane and enjoy the sights; but hours later she had seen so many shades of blue in the ocean below and flown through puffs of clouds for so long that her thoughts now centered on getting her feet back on the ground.

Resting her head on the window seat that she had previously felt so fortunate to be assigned, Cassandra Stevens noticed the dark blue upholstered seat held the odor of cleaning solution. The little pillow the flight attendant had given Cassie was, in her opinion, worthless.

As she closed her eyes for a few moments and considered what had brought her to this point in her life, her heart felt heavy with mixed emotions. Her mind was busy with thoughts of what lay ahead even though she was trying desperately to relax.

The makeup she had applied so many hours ago felt like a heavy mask. If Cassandra had not looked at herself in a compact mirror, she would've sworn it was actually dripping off of her face. She needed to relax. Closing her eyes, she envisioned the moment two hours hence when, after reaching her destination, she could get into a nice hot bath. She decided right then the bath would be full of bubbles with a cold glass of wine on the side as the finishing touch. In her mind's eye she saw the image of the bath, full of bubbles, and the chilled glass. She imagined little drops of moisture on the sides of the glass and she could almost feel the cold rim touching her lips. She let these thoughts capture her complete attention for a short while.

Cassandra was brought back to reality by a crying baby several rows behind her. Suddenly her head was again full of questions. Would there be any wine or a nice, big bath at the rental house? How would the house appear? Would she even want to take a bath there? Oh, what stupid thoughts, must be delirium, she told herself. Must relax, just relax, she silently chanted.

She could live without the wine, but there had at least better be a decent shower. She opened her eyes and laughed at herself and her thoughts. These are such silly, trivial needs. The company would not put her in a dump for the next several weeks. Cassie deeply wished the possible lack of wine and bubble bath were her only current problems.

As Cassie looked at her watch, she saw she still had forty-five minutes to go. She wished someone would get their baby to stop crying. Always, always, no matter where she was; in a restaurant, the doctor's office, wherever; she seemed to get seated around crying babies. Cassie then realized if she was tired of being cooped up in this plane, then the poor baby must really be exhausted. The child's incessant crying reminded Cassandra of her own children. Being away from them for so long was going to be very difficult for her. She wondered why people took young children on such a trip. Poor wailing child, poor exhausted parents, she thought as the cries seemed so much louder and more hollow in the cabin of the plane. Looking again at her watch, Cassie thought of how time must be dragging for all of them. With nothing but cloud puffs to look at out the window, she closed her eyes again and thought about her kids.

The high-pitched voice of one of the flight attendants came on the intercom and told the passengers to fasten their seat belts and secure all loose articles. At last they were preparing to land. This was always the best part of the flight to Cassandra. Watching the flight attendants hurry about among tired passengers looking for their properly assigned seats. She noticed overhead compartments being locked down and flight attendants visually checking seat belts. Just a little bit longer now, Cassandra thought.

Glancing out of the window she still saw nothing but clouds. Cassie knew that soon, very soon, she was going to look down at the bluest waters she had ever seen and tropical islands of lush green covered with exotic, aromatic flowers. But in spite of her excitement, Cassie longed to be sharing it with someone special.

Cassandra had always hoped she would be coming here with her husband; but, after 17 years of marriage they had never even had a real honeymoon. Cassie had always said it did not matter that she and her husband never had a real honeymoon. After all, she knew that the wedding ceremony and honeymoon did not make the marriage, but she always thought that one day it would be possible. Her husband had even come to Hawaii on three different business trips, but still could not afford for her to come along. And now here she was, on a business trip of her own, and without him. These days though, they never did much together. Cassandra considered the irony of being here, thinking of how they had never had a real honeymoon, and now, years later, it didn't look as though they would even share another anniversary.

She had to stop thinking of her personal problems and start preparing for the landing. There would be time to review her problems later. She was about to spend the next eight to twelve weeks in one of the most beautiful locations in the world, alone.

As the passengers came up the aisles to deplane, Cassie saw the toddler that had been doing all the crying. It had to be him, his eyes were wet with tears and he was still struggling to get out of his father's arms. Guessing the toddler to be about 18 to 20 months old, Cassandra reflected on her own children at that age. She knew she could never have held them in such a confined space for so long. Both of her kids love the outdoors and were adventurous tricksters. For them to sit still so long would have been pure torture for them.

At about that same age, Shane, her eldest, had gone behind the drapes in the bedroom one sunny afternoon. Cassie had spring cleaning fever and had opened windows to let the crisp fresh spring air inside the house. While she was cleaning, Shane repeatedly ran to the windows and looked out to see spring blossoming without him. After a while, he decided he wasn't going to wait any longer to go outside to play. So he pushed the screen out of the window and climbed out. A bit later Cassie had gone all over the house searching for him. She could hear him chattering to himself, but she could not find him. Throwing back the drapes, Cassie discovered the missing window screen. She leaned out the window to find Shane sitting there playing in the dirt. Feeling so relieved that he was all right, all she could do was run outside and grab him up. Covered in dirt, he had been having a great time playing by himself.

When Leigh, the youngest, was about 20 months old, she had pulled a similar stunt. Fortunately though, Cassie wasn't alone at the time, so she did not feel so much like she was losing her mind. Everyone in the house was looking for Leigh, under the beds, in the closets, everywhere.

At that time the kids had a little toy kitchen center in the play room. The kitchen center had a sink and cabinets, a little refrigerator, and colorful plastic toy food. Unknown to anyone, Leigh was just small enough that she could sit in the cabinet under the little sink and slide the cabinet door closed. After several minutes of frantic searching through the house, Shane said he could hear Leigh giggling in the play room. Cassie's parents were visiting that day and along with her they hurried to the play room, looked again in the closets and under the daybed; but still, no Leigh. Suddenly, the little door on the cabinet slid back and there sat the toddler, giggling about the trick she had just played on mommy. Cassie was so relieved and amused that all she could do was sit on the floor and laugh with Leigh. Shane, who was about five years old at the time, had suggested to his mom to take Leigh's picture while she sat in the cabinet. They got the camera and Leigh posed with a very proud and impish smile.

Until her niece was born, Cassandra had not been able to part with that particular piece of the children's toys. Every time she looked at it, she thought of how Leigh had giggled. She wanted to hold onto that memory forever. And now, when the memory came to mind, it brought with it both a smile and tears. How quickly they had grown. Cassie wondered how long her memories would hold her before she would have to see them.

Cassandra thought of a quote that she had once read. She didn't know the author, but she loved the quote. It went, "God gave us memories so we might have roses in December." Sometimes, Cassie felt memories were all she had, but they made a beautiful rose garden.

As the toddler and his parents came up the aisle by the row of seats where Cassandra stood waiting, she saw the anxious look in the faces of the parents. Cassie shook her head and said, "Poor baby, this trip has been trying for all of us. We can only imagine how hard it has been for this little one." Both the toddler's mom and dad smiled. Their smiles were of relief and gratitude that someone recognized how difficult it had been for their baby. The dad offered to let Cassandra out into the aisle and she politely declined. She said she would do nothing to make that poor baby wait any longer. Actually, Cassandra was trying to get herself together before she deplaned and met the company associate who was to pick her up and drive her to the rented house. Cassie worked very hard at appearing to have it all together, even when she was crumbling on the inside. And this evening, even after the long grueling plane trip, she would step off appearing completely intact.

As she walked the ramp between the plane and the building, Cassie thought about the native Hawaiians who used to greet visitors with the orchid leis. But they didn't do that anymore. Oh, the leis were there if you wanted one, but you had to buy it from one of the many vendors set up in the airport. Everything had a price, even in paradise.

Chapter 3

A
T FIRST CASSIE was surprised at how many people were
attired in the traditional flowered Hawaiian shirts and
dresses, but she liked the casual, comfortable atmosphere.
A young man, dressed in dark slacks and a white shirt, stood
out against all the flowered shirts and khaki cargo shorts.
Cassandra wondered if he was Todd Sievers, the company
associate who was to pick her up at the airport. The young
man kept glancing over at Cassie, but would then look away
and continue to search the people still coming off of the plane.

Cassandra continued to look over the crowd already waiting
there and finally decided to give the local office a call on her cell
phone to be sure someone was coming for her. As she spoke
to a woman at the office named Carla, she looked around for
the individual that Carla was describing to her. He was 26, tall
and slender, with dark blond hair, fair skin and wire-rimmed
glasses. Cassie asked if she thought Todd would be dressed in
the native attire. Carla laughed and said, "No, no, Todd is all
business. Most likely he will be wearing dark slacks and a light-
colored shirt and maybe even a tie." Cassandra knew then, the
young man who had been discreetly observing her was Todd
Sievers. She thanked Carla and said she hoped to meet her
within the next few days, but now she thought she had spotted
Todd and would have to get off the phone.

The young man turned around and looked surprised to see
Cassie approaching him. The closer she got, the more he prepared himself to say, "Mrs. Stevens?" Even though Todd had
tried, he was not capable of concealing the surprise in his

voice. Cassandra knew that most people were surprised by her appearance and men especially seemed to have a difficult time with her having good looks and intelligence. But Todd was young and open-minded and now, he was privately looking forward to this working experience. He had not counted on Cassandra Stevens being a woman who was breathtakingly beautiful.

There were times when Cassie enjoyed watching people's reactions to her. Other times, with men and women, she found her appearance both a hindrance and worrisome. This particular evening, on her first encounter with someone from the local office, she wanted only to appear as all business. She would not reveal how tired she was and she certainly wouldn't show her fun-loving, girlish side. Cassie knew how much first impressions counted and she was determined to come across as mature, intelligent and very capable. She knew the first impression Todd perceived of her could determine how well the other people at the local office worked with her.

It was late in the day and Cassandra still wanted that bubble bath. After shaking Todd's hand and introducing herself, she took the lead and began to move toward the baggage claim area. While waiting for her luggage, Cassie decided to break the ice and drop some of the formality. She told Todd she was very tired and she hoped the house the company had sub leased for her wasn't too far away. Todd smiled and replied that no drive on the island lasted for very long. Cassie laughed slightly and realized she should have thought of that herself. Perhaps she was more tired than she was aware.

As Cassandra's luggage came around on the carousel, she leaned over to reach for it, only to find Todd trying to reach over her to get it before her. She smiled at the realization that chivalry wasn't dead. Even though she was ten years his senior, Todd was trying to be a gentleman by not letting her lift the heavy luggage. There were times Cassie would have liked to have dropped all barriers and allowed some very strong and masculine man to take over for her. But then she wondered how long she could deal with not thinking for herself and moving by her own instincts.

As they waited for Cassie's second piece of luggage, she felt Todd was looking her over. He was. Todd was admiring the full head of glossy blonde hair cascading over the shoulders of this shapely body, and when Cassie turned to say something to him, he was struck by her peachy young complexion. Todd felt she had the most perfect lips; not too full, not narrow, but perfect. When she spoke, her emerald green eyes seemed to say as much as her mouth. She didn't have any age lines in her face, only one little laugh line that Todd thought to be an attribute. He found that even though she was dressed in a conservative way, Cassandra carried an aura about her that said she was all woman, a very sexy woman. Todd decided this job assignment was going to be much more intriguing than he had first thought.

While putting Cassandra's baggage in the trunk of his car, Todd told her one of the secretaries at the local office had seen to it that the rented house had everything she might need, including some food items. He then offered to take her to dinner somewhere so she wouldn't have to cook during her first night. Cassie thanked him as they got into the car, saying that, if he did not mind, she would like to take a rain check, as tonight she just wanted to get settled in and prepare for tomorrow. She considered Todd's thoughtfulness, for he probably had a girlfriend whom he would rather have taken to dinner tonight. As Cassie smiled at Todd she thought how cute he was, in a bookworm sort of way. He was tall and lean, certainly not a bodybuilder or surfer type. By his fair complexion she guessed that, even though he was surrounded by some of the most beautiful beaches, he spent little time on them. She liked the way his wire-rimmed glasses suited his face, for they made him appear to be even more sensitive and thoughtful than he had already indicated.

During the drive along the ocean highway, Cassandra was speechless as the road continually dipped into lush ravines with exotic flowers that held colors she had never witnessed before. Honolulu was as lovely as its name. Todd said Hawaii was rich in history and tradition and as soon as she wanted to do some sightseeing he would take her for a drive along Diamond Head Road where it forked at Kahala Avenue. He pointed out that along this strip were the homes of the rich and famous on the island of Oahu. Cassie was so excited she was afraid to speak, fearing she would sound more giddy than she was already.

There were people everywhere on mopeds and bicycles. The white sand beaches were dotted with tanned bodies and brightly colored swimsuits. She saw women dressed in the colorful Hilo Hattie dresses. There were tall palm trees and healthy, muscular horses grazing on lush green, knee-high grasses underneath them. Cassie actually shrieked when she saw a landscape crew mowing the natural growing orchids.

Cassie remembered the time when her husband, Dale, had come home from one of his trips to Hawaii and brought her and the kid's samples of the Hawaiian attire. When Leigh put on her red and white Hilo Hattie dress, she looked like she belonged on the island, for Cassandra was part American Indian, but the only physical indication of her heritage were her high cheekbones. Leigh had the long, dark hair and she and Shane were both dark complected. All they had to do to get a tan was to walk outside in the sun. Shane had gotten a sea foam green island shirt with black palm trees on it and he looked like he had just come from the Big Island. Cassie's husband had brought her a periwinkle and white Hilo Hattie dress. Cassie fell in love with it right away, not only because of the color or the comfort of the dress, but because it was, in all their years of marriage, the first article of clothing Dale had ever given her. It was a moment she knew she would never forget.

Lost in the beauty of the passing scenery and her own personal thoughts, Cassandra suddenly realized Todd was speaking to her. While she had been admiring the scenery of the land, Todd had been admiring her. He had noted the way she walked, the way she sat, the way she turned her head, everything about her commanded respect in a soft, yet determined way. The fact she had spoken very little to Todd made it difficult for him to determine whether she was an airhead or shy or just didn't speak unless she had something worth saying. He had even been savoring the scent of her perfume, for he wanted to remember that fragrance forever.

Todd told Cassandra he had met her husband, Dale, on two of his trips to Hawaii. Then he laughed and said maybe one day the company would find a way to send them both over at the same time. Cassie laughed a little and said she certainly hoped he was right, but in her heart she was wondering if she and Dale would stay together long enough to see it happen. Oh Dale, Cassie thought, did he even know how much he hurt her? Or had Cassie portrayed herself even to him as capable and responsible, to the point he thought she did not need him? There were so many unanswered questions, so many raw nerves.

Chapter 4

O NCE, WHEN TIMOTHY was about eight, his mother took him with her on a trip to Europe. He didn't want to go. She brought it up at the dinner table one evening. His dad made it clear he did not have the time to go, no matter when she set the date. Upsetting his mother with such a broad, but unspoken "no"; she sat there and silently fumed for a few minutes. Then she spoke up again and said "That's okay. Your son and I will go and have a fun time with just the two of us."

The little boy shot a glance to his dad, his eyes pleading for his father to intervene, to give her a blunt no for him going as well, but his father did not. Instead he just smiled at his wife and said, "Well if you think that is what you want to do, then go ahead and book your trip." The boy's heart sank, for he knew he would be all alone in a strange place with a woman who did not care about his happiness at all, it was all about her.

For the next two weeks Timothy fretted over the possibility his mother would really take him on such a trip, and his dad stay behind. That would leave him alone with her, for who knows how long, and without his hiding place to run to for security. To even think about it gave him the shivers.

When the third week came around, his mother caught him coming in the door from school one day and told him to put his books away, they were going shopping. Timothy tried to feign excitement when he asked what they were going to shop for, but when his mother turned and glared at him, he wished he'd never spoken.

As they entered the first department store, he knew it was probably for clothes for him, and when his mother spoke to the clerk, he felt his heart faint. Suddenly all the air was gone from his lungs. She told the clerk she needed a full week's worth of new clothes for her son for a trip abroad. She said she could have them cleaned each week while they were at different locations, but she could not go over to Europe with him looking like such a ragamuffin. The clerk laughed a little, not sure if she was serious or trying to be funny. Then the clerk began his questions with where abroad do you plan on going, just so he could determine the climate and start putting some outfits together for her son to wear.

The boy's mother put on airs, like she doesn't exactly know where all they will go, but plan on the climate being most similar to that of England. Yes, England, for they would probably spend more time there than anywhere else. And, she went on telling the clerk, she could always buy him more clothes once there, wherever they went, but she needed a suitcase full of new stuff to get him started. The clerk fell for it completely. All he saw before him was a woman with a full pocketbook and him getting a nice commission check at the end of the week. He never saw the boy, and the anguish in his small face.

The little boy followed the clerk around the boys department completely without expression. The clerk quickly gathered up sets of clothes with socks to match, and then a sweater and a jacket. After pulling a couple of packages of boys underwear he turned to the boy's mother and asked if she would like him to also take them over to the shoe department for a couple of pairs of matching shoes. She said of course, whatever the child needed, get it done. Still, the clerk was so happy knowing he had an open tab to fill, making his commission check even greater, he never noticed the sad, lost little boy who obediently followed him around the store.

Four hours later they returned to their home. The boy's mother looked at him, told him to go to his room and get on his homework. She said she would have the maid launder and pack his new things, and the cook would bring him something to eat in a bit, but for now, leave her site, she had seen enough of him for one day. Timothy was not shocked by the way she spoke to him, this was normal to him. He wanted to ask questions about the trip abroad that they had just been shopping for, but knew it was a waste of time. She would only tell him the day they were due to leave. He slowly made his way up the spiraling stairs to his room. He welcomed the quiet darkness of that room. He had seen enough of her for one day, too.

Chapter 5

H IS MOTHER WAS a big built woman, red hair, and always cut in a page boy style, with very little variation. She wore straight skirts, sometimes with a matching jacket. She thought she appeared to be a professional. She was very domineering, and thought she knew everything, even though she never finished college. Even then she thought she knew more than the educators and it was a waste of her time.

Her family was wealthy and she flaunted their wealth every time she got the opportunity. When her parents passed, they left her with three banks and real estate all over the state of New York. She felt it was owed her, for she had tolerated years of abuse by her father. He put on a great front as a well established, distinguished business man, but when he got home, he was a pervert, and it was his daughter he went after. She always felt her mother had to know, but chose to ignore so as to not affect the lifestyle she loved to live.

Her mother booked evenings out with friends, playing cards, going to the movies, women's club meetings, anything so she would be gone in the evenings. She knew that was when her husband had his way with their daughter, and it made it easier if she were gone for her to tolerate the knowledge of what was really going on in her home. Most often when she did come home, her husband and daughter would be gone. Her husband always took their daughter out for treats after he had had his way with her, it was a "pay off, hush treat". He thought his money would take care of the damage he inflicted on his daughter as well as keep his wife quiet and out of the way. The little girl began to just accept it as the way of life, unaware of how wrong it was. It would be years later before she was aware of just how she had been abused. Mentally, physically, emotionally and sexually. It would leave an open wound in her heart wider than the Atlantic for the remainder of her life.

So, now she was a mother and after years of abuse, the ugliness just seemed to get spread around. She had never received professional help, no one, no one could ever know what her prestigious father had done, or that her mother willingly ignored it. Now it was her burden of shame to carry throughout her life. The family money would now have to pave golden roads in front of her, and others, strangers, would have to bend at her will. She was a woman full of hate.

It was her nature to be hateful to others, especially for people who worked in service positions. She felt her stature gave her the right to be condescending and order people around. She would look people in the eye and lie about anything and everything. Lying came easy to her, as did acting, for she had lived a life of acting, her entire childhood had been an act. What she felt towards her family was pure hatred, but she enjoyed their money. Their money was what got her a good husband, a younger man, who used her family money to start his own business, which eventually became so financially sound that he had attained more wealth than her family.

It was around that time her husband decided to leave her, for he could no longer take her hatefulness, towards him, their son, the house staff, and people in general. He had put up with a lot, smiling at people when she was ugly to them, hoping his smile would soften the pain she inflicted with her words, but knowing full well she was an arrogant, hateful bitch. He could not even remember a time when she had a natural smile, everything was a front, it was all fake.

When he left, he did not take their son. He knew his wife physically and verbally abused their son. He claimed the long hours he worked to build their empire was so he could leave it to his son. The real truth was he had a new woman in his life. She was younger and wanted them to start their own family, and he couldn't wait to leave the ugly tyrant bitch he was currently married to behind. She could keep her banks, her land, her manipulating ways, her ignorant egotistical attitude, everything, he just wanted to get out. He was leaving the old, worn out bully for someone younger, fresh and sweet. Someone who wanted him.

His first son would have to wait. He would just have to endure, as he had done for so many years. Even though he was an adult, he failed to realize his son did not choose to be in that environment, he was a child born into a hellhole. It was his father who chose to marry into that family, he knew what he was getting himself into, so to rationalize his son would just have to endure as he had was ludicrous, he was being a selfish, irresponsible parent, again.

Chapter 6

R EALIZING TODD WAS speaking to her again, Cassie tuned into what he was saying. He was telling her how happy everyone at the Honolulu office was to have been awarded this government contract and how everyone there wanted her to know, if she needed anything at all, she was to let them know and they would see it was done. Cassie thanked him, but she also got the feeling the people in the local office might be questioning whether or not she was the right "man" for the job.

Todd went on to confirm her suspicions by asking her if she knew how big the job really was and in what kind of facility she would be working? Cassandra told him she knew exactly what kind of facility it was and felt her previous work history was part of the reason the company gave the job to her. She also stated she felt the company had plenty of people they could have chosen to do the job, yet they chose her, so they must have deemed her capable. Todd uttered that he did not mean she was incapable, saying only that, well, it was a prison facility, an all-male prison, and he was surprised the company had chosen a woman. He said he meant no offense, but he just felt it might be very uncomfortable for her. Cassie assured him no offense was taken. She went on to tell Todd that two years previously she had worked for the State Bureau of Prisons in a contract position. She had the background clearance, with the exception of the last two years, which made it easier for the government to check her out; not to mention that she knew how the system worked, making it easier on the company. She was aware of the stress involved and knew how to deal with the prison system.

Even more intrigued with Cassandra, Todd told her he was not aware of her past work history. Then he admitted to Cassie that, when he first saw her at the airport, he knew she could not be the one, for the company would never have sent such an attractive woman to work at an all-male prison. They both laughed and Cassie thanked him for the compliment, saying that, after so many hours on the plane, it was certainly a welcomed compliment. Todd smiled as he thought to himself of how much he already liked what he knew of Cassandra Stevens. She was not only beautiful and pleasant, but she was human, and a gloriously beautiful human with whom he was going to enjoy the time he got to spend.

For a few moments there was silence in the car. Cassandra withdrew into thoughts of her own as she considered what had been said. Compliments. Two years ago, when she had worked at the prison, she got more compliments than she knew what to do with. The two and half years she had been employed by the system had certainly opened her eyes as 1100 inmates continually told Cassie how nice she was, how beautiful, and how lucky her husband was and so on. She was always respectful of the inmates, she did not know their history, only that they were human like her. Yes, she had learned a lot while working there; about herself, her husband, the prison system and the government. It was part of the reason she had left when she did. She found she could no longer hide her fears or her vulnerability. Cassandra had learned enough to become fearful; fearful of herself, and the government.

When she finally got the courage to leave the prison system, she had also made up her mind that, regardless of her future position, she was going to be somebody. She had achieved her goal in a much shorter time than even she had imagined. In thinking back, Cassie wondered if she had worked even harder in an attempt to leave the past behind. There was a lot she wanted to forget. It wasn't her style to turn her back on what she considered improper, but she knew that most people would not believe what she had witnessed at the prison. She had tried to discuss it rationally with her husband time and time again until he began to just tune her out. Dale knew there was nothing they could do about circumstances at the prison.

The general public was not sympathetic towards inmates; but, the general public was not aware of the differences between the prison systems either. Cassandra was not aware until she was employed there. She was horrified by some of the incidents she witnessed and the dramatic differences in the guidelines. But, more than that, she was dismayed by the apparent innocence of the public while paying tax dollars to support a system which did not work, for the taxpayers or the inmates.

It worked for those who were making the system their career, whether they were agents in the field, staff, or guards at the prison. That was not to say she felt the system as a whole wasn't necessary, but there was plenty of room for improvement. Nor was it to say the people who work for the government were all looking for an easy paycheck but, as in any situation, it only took a few bad apples to spoil the whole barrel. Cassie had seen plenty of bad apples. Any who were good usually left, or were soon spoiled, which said to Cassie there was probably a flaw in their character anyway. She had left to put it all behind because she knew alone she could not fight it. She was afraid of sounding like a fanatic, so she left.

Now, her new career was sitting her right down in the middle of the prison system again; but, this time she was going to be the one doing the tuning out. Cassandra Stevens would see or do nothing more than focus on her job for the next few weeks and then she would leave it all behind once again. She said a silent prayer for strength.

It was at that moment when Todd turned the car into a driveway. Cassie gave way to a small gasp at the beauty of the house. It sat up on the hill and only clouds could be seen behind it. The driveway was lined with palm trees and as they approached the house, Cassandra was made speechless by the gorgeous flower beds. They were planted with orchids, rows and rows of deep red and purple orchids. As she stepped out of the car, Cassie stood and inhaled the aroma of the flowers and the scented air.

She turned and looked past the house to see the ocean behind it, for she had also smelled salt water. She had no idea the home would be so lovely nor even at the ocean's edge. Staying here was going to be a dream come true and, once again, Cassie thought of her family. Somehow she would get them to come out and join her. If her husband could not or would not come, then she would still have the children. This would be such a treat for them, as well.

Chapter 7

A S TODD UNLOCKED the front door to the leased house, he turned to Cassandra and asked her if she was going to be afraid staying out here by herself? Saying if she was, he felt the company wouldn't mind her staying at a hotel instead, so long as she was comfortable. Cassie assured him she was looking forward to the quiet solitude and the house would be perfect. Todd pushed the door back and then went to get her luggage out of the car. Cassie stepped inside the house, but did not venture away from the doorway.

The house was big and open with lots of Italian tile and huge plate glass windows. The furnishings were not crowded, but not sparse either. Everything was in its place, and it all appeared well kept and clean. And to think Cassie was wondering if it would even have a bath tub! Now she couldn't wait to see the size of that bathtub. She knew the contract she was working here was valuable to the company, but she had never imagined staying at such an impressive place.

Todd stepped past Cassandra, carrying her three pieces of luggage to one of the guest bedrooms. He turned on lights as he went through the house and Cassie sensed he had been here before. She remained near the door. She felt Todd was nice enough, but she did not know anything about him, and she was aware there was not another house for some distance. One thing for sure, working at the prison had taught her to be cautious.

Todd came back through the house explaining to Cassie that the house belonged to a wealthy older couple who traveled to

Europe every year for three or four months. They did not like to leave the house unoccupied for such a long period of time so they leased it out to certain businesses for their executives stay while on the island. The maid and gardener would continue to come on their regular schedule and they were aware Cassandra would be staying there for several weeks. If there were any problems with the house, she had only to pick up the phone and call the local office in Honolulu.

Todd again said everyone at the corporate office was aware of her presence and the job she had to do here and they wanted her to be happy and content. It was also where he had his office and he would be delighted to assist her in any way. Cassie commented he seemed to know his way around the house and he laughed. Todd admitted he and another coworker had brought out the rental car earlier in the day and had put it away in the garage. They had also brought her a basket of fruit from the office, which she would find on the breakfast table. While there they could not resist looking through the house.

Softly laughing, Todd said they were just as awestruck as she apparently was, for she had not moved away from the door since they had arrived. Cassie laughed as well and put her behavior off to jet lag and being awestruck, too. For she did not want to hurt Todd's feelings, but she was not taking any chances either. Todd started to leave, then he told Cassandra the keys to the car were on the table by the fruit basket and that, when she had rested and was ready to do some sightseeing, to just give him a call because he would be happy to show her around. Cassie thanked him for everything and he left. She locked the door and turned to look around, and suddenly felt how immense the house was and almost wished Todd hadn't left.

Cassandra walked down the entryway, looking from side to side as she went. The big white Italian tile made the house appear even larger and gave it clean lines. She noted the sofas and fresh flowers, the huge area rug in the living room, wall hangings, everything, was done in soft and light hues of pink and aqua. The whole living area looked more like a watercolor painting done in lovely pastels. The walls were almost all glass, with blinds that she could open and close with a remote. There was a sense of peace and contentment here, and this was just what Cassie needed. She walked on into the kitchen and saw the basket of fruit and the car keys on the breakfast table. She picked up the car keys and put the house key Todd had given her on the same key ring, then she dropped it into the outside pocket of her purse. She didn't want a lot of loose ends tomorrow morning, so she would take care of little things like keys tonight.

Cassie pulled an orange out of the basket, changed her mind, took an apple instead and looked out the plate glass windows behind the table. Outside there was a huge patio, and the backyard tiered off into several different levels until it reached the beaches below. There were steps at each level, lined with more of the colorful flowers. The patio had an outdoor table and chairs and at each corner sat a huge flowerpot; but, rather than more flowers, the pots contained pepper, tomato and green onion plants. Cassandra was intrigued, but decided to wait and explore outside one afternoon before dark. Still being cautious, she elected to contain her exploring to the inside of the house tonight.

Walking from room to room, Cassie was enjoying each one more than the other. She didn't know the age of the owners; but, it was obvious by the home decor and furnishings they thought young. Everything was done very tastefully, with nothing cluttered, overpowering or outdated. It was perfect. Cassie wondered how often the owners called in an interior designer to update the house, or if it was their own good taste and judgment that made this place so beautiful. Regardless, she loved it.

As she walked into the on-suite bathroom, she held her breath, waiting to see the bath she had dreamed of a couple of hours earlier on the plane. It was more than she had ever imagined. The bath was big enough for two people and more than that, there was an assortment of bubble baths and bath beads lined up on the side in glass jars that looked like a miniature set of canisters. Behind the bath was a half circle atrium full of tropical greenery and the wall behind the atrium was made of glass brick so that during the day the sun could feed the greenery and bathroom with natural light. The clear glass shower was as expansive as the tub with four shower heads and a built-in tile bench so the bather could either sit or lay on it. Cassie found herself moving to sit down on the side of the tub as she continued to take in the beauty of this room. The dressing area was separate from the bath and there was a lovely vanity just off the lavatories.

Above each dressing area were huge skylights which also peaked over the three-quarter high walls between the dressing area and the closets. This allowed the natural sunlight to peek in and help in picking and matching colors of clothes and shoes in the closets. Along the top of the three-quarter high walls ran the prettiest ivy plants Cassandra had ever seen. The whole bathroom was done in white marble, glass and bronze. For a few moments she just sat. She was grateful there wasn't anyone there to see her reaction to the house. She was dumbfounded and this was not the image for which the "controlled" Cassandra Stevens wanted to be known. She would be staying in the guest side of the house, separate from the owner's master bedroom and bath. This suited Cassie just fine as she would not have to feel like she was invading someone's privacy.

When she collected herself, she thought of how she could not wait to tell her family, and then she thought of her husband. What a perfect place to have that long overdue honeymoon!

Maybe not; maybe it was better to enjoy it alone. Maybe it was time for her to have an affair. After all, she often wondered if he had. Stop thinking like this, she told herself. Without a doubt it was time for her to go and see if she could complete her earlier image with a glass of wine. Dredging up such haunting thoughts brought on the need for a glass of wine.

In the game room, Cassie looked behind the bar to find more than one bottle of wine in the chiller. She made a mental note to buy some wine to replace it one day when she was out. Even the game room was glorious, reflecting the same pink and aqua hues, but in a playful flower print. This house cried out for people to enjoy it and that was just what Cassie intended to do.

With her wine glass in hand, Cassie went back to the bath and started the water. She picked the bubble bath she wanted, and poured some in the bath. Cassie knew she picked it because it had the fragrance of fresh peaches and reminded her of home.

As the water ran in the tub, Cassie walked into the bedroom where Todd had put her luggage. There was a king size bed, a desk and a chaise lounge that were once again, simple but elegant. She opened one of the suitcases and got a robe and gown and went back to check the bath water. She realized this bath was going to take quite a bit of water to fill the tub.

Then she thought she heard the house phone ringing. Quickly she moved into the bedroom and answered the phone. It was Todd. He said when he got home he realized he had failed to give her his home and cell phone numbers and had also forgotten to explain the burglar alarm to her. As he told her the alarm code he also told her about the red emergency button in each room. Cassie looked at the wall and there, by the headboard of the bed, was a red button on a switch plate. She knew these buttons would alert the local emergency teams if pushed, for she had learned about them at a friend's lake house years before. Cassie thanked Todd and quickly got off the phone and ran to check the bathwater. It was still not full enough and she added some more bubble bath. She smiled to herself as she went to set the burglar alarm and thought how this was going to be more like swimming in bubbles than taking a bath. She could hardly wait to get undressed and step in the tub. At last, she was going to wash off the makeup mask and bring her earlier dream into reality.

A half-hour later Cassandra was peeling herself out of the deep bath and, dropping the towel from her head she watched in one of the many mirrors as her hair cascaded around her shoulders. She continued to towel herself dry and while she wrapped the towel around her, continued to look in the mirrors that surrounded the bathroom. Even at 36 years of age she was still attractive. She had made the decision years before to always take good care of herself. Because she felt so strongly about age being a state of mind, she thought young, acted young, felt young, and definitely appeared young. Her thick blond hair dropped just past her shoulders, and her smooth skin, big green eyes and high cheekbones did not necessitate the use of makeup, but Cassandra felt at times, one should improve on what one had. She could use her hair and makeup to perfect her appearance, in different ways to accomplish just about anything. She was not totally unaware of her good looks; she just did not abuse them or use them in an attempt to hurt anyone.

Only with her two pregnancies did she gain weight, but she quickly lost the baby weight and had maintained a wonderful figure from there on. Standing there naked, fresh and clean, she wondered why her husband had felt the need to emotionally abandon her. She wasn't a boring individual, she was always interested in his work, and she certainly was not illiterate. What had she ever done, or not done, to deserve being hurt like that by someone she loved so completely? The tears began to silently roll down her cheeks. She quickly shook it off and told herself she needed to get to bed, she needed rest.

Chapter 8

L ISTENING TO THE PHONE ring on the other end, Cassie could hardly wait to hear the voices of her children. She would not let on to her husband she had been thinking about the emotional pain he caused her. If he answered, she would come across as happy and excited and act as though she could not wait for him and the kids to join her out here. The little voice on the other end answered and Cassie knew it was Leigh. Even though the kids sounded the same on the phone to most people, if you listened just right, there was a little tweak in Leigh's voice that was not apparent in Shane's; but then, only a mother would recognize it. "Hi Baby!" "Mom! Are you there? What's the house like? Tell me it's not a dump, Mom, please." "No, Baby, it's not a dump, it is really very, very nice and I cannot wait for you guys to come out here!" As Cassie talked, Leigh was trying to relay everything to the others until Shane took the phone away. "Hi Mom!" Cassie politely scolded Shane for crowding in on his little sister and after he made some vague excuse about Leigh always hogging the phone, they got on with the conversation about Hawaii, the plane trip and the rental house.

The kids were proud of their mom. They had watched her grow almost as much as she had watched them. Cassie had personally sacrificed a lot to earn their love and trust and they had not failed her. They were not only her children, they were her best friends, her allies.

After a few minutes, Cassie told Shane to put Leigh back on the phone. They discussed school, the plane trip, and Cassie told Leigh about the toddler on the plane and how it made her remember the time that she had hidden in the toy cabinet. They both laughed and Leigh said "I miss you already, Mom. I love you so much." Shane pulled the phone away again and hollered in the receiver, "I love you, too, Mom!" Cassie laughed, declared her love for both of them and then asked them to put their dad on the phone.

After a few moments, she heard Dale say "Hi there! How was the trip out there?" It seemed all their conversations stayed on topics or current events these days. When Cassandra finally got around to asking Dale about him and the kids coming out to Hawaii, he gave a weak reply, saying that he would check out everyone's schedules and get back with her. Cassie smiled wanly as she thought of how during her orientation at the prison she had been instructed her safest answers to an inmate were either a flat "No" or "let me get back with you.", thus giving the staff person time to consider what had been asked. The idea was that, when a staff person is given a few seconds to consider the question, the inmate had nothing but time to figure out how to ask the question to get what they wanted. Such occasions had rarely surfaced for Cassie with 1100 inmates; but, for her husband, this was a common reply to her. She would give it some time and see if he did work something out or if he even grew to miss her. After all, it's said, "Absence makes the heart grow fonder."

Chapter 9

THE HOUSE HE lived in was interesting. He had purchased a duplex, each side having two bedrooms and two bathrooms. Not what you would have expected a man with his education and background to be living in, for he could afford so much more. But he claimed it was so one side would always be clean and ready for friends and family who came to visit from the mainland, even though he knew there was no one who would ever come.

If someone did ask to come over or drop something by, he would give them the address for the side of the duplex where no one lived. Completely furnished, with fine leather sofas and teak wood tables, he could give the appearance of keeping a nice, clean home. The truth was, the other half of the duplex, where he really lived, he surrounded himself with his personal little oddities. Pictures of women he didn't know, but liked their appearance. Women he had spotted on the beach or in the market. He was a watcher, not a participant. In some cases he would have maps posted by their pictures of how to get to their homes or apartments. He was a stalker who never intended to get close to the ones he was stalking, but in his mind, he was building a life with them. He would imagine if they would have kids, what kind of house they would live in, and would they have a cat or a dog, etc. He wanted to know what it was like, but never trusted himself to share his feelings with anyone else, so he lived inside of himself.

Sometimes the loneliness at home would eat him alive with memories. Bad memories, so he would often frequent a couple of local eateries that had a bar and televisions where he could view the pro-sports games taking place that day. He preferred to sit in the bar side of the restaurant. For one, he liked the smell of the beer coming off the taps, the clinking of the glasses. Second, to be away from families, especially families with children. He avoided the main dining area because he did not want to hear parents with their kids, consider what it might be like, or possibly to realize what he truly missed out on as a child himself.

Couples made him think about his never ending loneliness. Families with children made him think about his own childhood. Sitting in the bar area of a restaurant was not, to him, like sitting in a bar or club all alone. He enjoyed pro-sports games and being around others, hearing them yell out with excitement made him feel like he had a somewhat normal life. But his normal life was only in his mind, for in reality, his life was the polar opposite.

The one thing that bothered him about one of the restaurants he frequented was a particular man and his wife who always seem to show up after work. He had watched them for several months and their routine never wavered. They came in like clockwork and always drank like fish. The husband was a short man, fat as a tick, and very loud and obnoxious. He acted like he owned the place, but it was obvious by the way they dressed, and the manner in which they carried themselves, they didn't have much. Cheap clothes and absolutely no class. The husband would engage in conversation with anyone who looked his way, the wife just sat and drank. She always smiled and laughed at the appropriate times, but her interest was purely in the beer she was holding at that moment.

On more than one occasion the husband had tried to strike up a conversation with him, but he would brush him off. The management could see how annoying he was to customers, but for whatever the reason, they tolerated his loud, out spoken behavior. Ignoring him was becoming a chore, so time to move to the other restaurant/bar for a while. *Mr. No Class Drunk* and his beer guzzling, big butted wife were too much for him.

One afternoon, shortly after five, he stopped into his second favorite restaurant/bar. He seated himself at the bar, ordered some dinner and a cold beer, and began watching a basketball game on one of the big screen televisions. Very much into the game and just ordering his second beer, he heard a loud commotion behind him. He turned to see the short, fat man and his big butted wife entering the bar. All he could think was, it's barely six in the evening and these two were stumbling in, already half drunk, and once again, acting like they own this place, too. He knew then he would be getting his dinner to go and leaving.

The fat little man and his big butted wife sat at a table near the windows and the waiter approached them, only to have the man shout at the Bartender, "Jake, you know what we want, I'm not tipping a damn waiter!" The Bartender waved and said, "Coming right out!" The waiter went behind the bar to see what he could do to help, and he heard the waiter ask the Bartender, "Is this the guy you told me about?" The Bartender nodded and said "I will take his beers to him, they'll be here drinking all evening."

The waiter stayed behind the bar watching, so he struck up a conversation with him saying, "What's the story with those two?" The young waiter kind of smirked and said, "The husband works for one of the major beer distributors and he thinks the local bars and restaurants like him and he's always looking for free food and beer. He and his wife show up somewhere different in town almost every night and the managers are afraid to offend him because he threatens he can delay their beer deliveries at the very worst of times. They're both obnoxious drunks and mooches. The owner hates it when they come in here cause they think they're special and as you saw, think no one but management should wait on them. Truth is, I bet the beer company he represents has no idea how he abuses his position and their company name."

Listening to the waiter, he said, "You're probably right about that, lucky they haven't been in an accident or picked up for drunk in public." The young waiter just responded with, "Yeah, but sooner or later, everyone's number comes up." With that they just smiled at each other, and his dinner arrived. He sat his empty beer mug down on the brightly colored tile bar, took the sack with the to-go box inside and prepared to leave.

Suddenly, the fat little man was standing beside him. He said, "I've seen you before, but you never talk to us, what's up with that?" He laughed slightly and said, "Nothing personal, just got other things to do." "Ha, not good enough! Come have a beer with us, I'll buy!" With that he saw the young waiter smirk again. "Thanks, but another time." After he went back to his table to join his wife, the Bartender turned to him and apologized. He said "The beer distributor he works for has no idea how he represents them and abuses their reputation and we honestly do not know what to do about him. He only cares about how much he and his wife can drink and act like they own the place. We are sick of them." He just kind of shook his head in disbelief of what he was being told, put down a tip and turned to leave.

As he started across the bar, the wife, once again sitting and drinking by herself, looked right up at him and gave him a weak, sheepish smile. It was the first time she had looked right at him, the very first time he had seen her crystal blue eyes. Blue like glaciers, icy cold glaciers. He laughed to himself as he walked on wondering if the color of her eyes matched her personality.

Chapter 10

O NE NIGHT LATE, as they both stumbled out of the restaurant, falling into the tropical plants and wooden tables as they crossed the bar, they were unaware of the disapproving looks being shot at them by the different folks still in the restaurant bar, both employees and customers. The fat little man was as usual, obnoxious, loud and rude. Worst of all, he thought he was funny and everyone wanted to hear his dumb stories. If only he knew how he had worn out his welcome, all over town.

His ignorant, low class wife was just there for the beer, and in her own small mind, thought he was somebody. Every now and then, she would feign a phony laugh to keep him amused, but even she was tired of his stupid stories, so she would just amuse herself with another beer.

Together they rounded the corner of the building to the parking lot in the rear, away from the main street of traffic, with him complaining he should never have to park in the back parking lot. Caught totally unaware and unprepared, a man stepped out of the shadows and with a quick slice through the air, he slit the throat of the fat butted wife. In an instant he turned to her prick of a husband and said, "No more beer for you, Bozo!" and he slit his throat with the same quick, silent motion, quietly laughing as the man took the short fall to the ground with a look of horror on his face. The assailant moved ever so quickly around the man and back to the big butted wife. He knelt over her now lifeless body, laid a small box on the ground beside her head, and proceeded with expert precision to remove her crystal blue eyes. "You don't need these anymore. They will go well with my collection. Hope you enjoyed your beer tonight."

Then he heard a voice behind him asking, "What happened? What's wrong with them?" Still kneeling over the fat butted woman, he looked back and saw a young woman who sometimes joined them and drank as much as they did. He quickly responded with, "I don't know, I just came around the corner and found them like this! Do you know them?" Quickly she answered, "She's my friend!" She knelt down beside him, and as soon as she could see the woman's eyes were missing, he grabbed her around the neck and said, "Stupid is as Stupid does, and now you can join them in hell!" With those final words he slit her throat as quietly and easily as he did theirs. He rose, looked at the three bodies lying there together and smiled to himself. And as quickly as he moved in on them, he was gone into the darkness.

Their bodies were found a short time later by workers leaving the restaurant. They weren't even cold yet. The police were mystified, the public was horrified. Their killer was happy.

Chapter 11

CASSANDRA WAS UP early her first morning. Having been so tired the night before, she had gone to bed with only an apple and a glass of wine for dinner and this morning she awoke feeling hungry. She took a quick shower and lavished in the glory of the four shower heads. After drying her hair and making up her mind on what she would wear the first morning, which she decided would be black slacks and a crisp white blouse, she hurried into the kitchen to see what she could find for breakfast.

Much to her surprise, she found the maid. The house was so big she hadn't even heard the maid cleaning at the other end. The maid offered to scramble her some eggs and serve it with toast and fresh fruit from the basket. Cassandra gratefully accepted, not that she couldn't prepare it herself; but, it would not take as long to get done with someone who knew their way around the kitchen and she did not want to show up late this first morning.

Cassie hurried back to the bedroom to get her briefcase, all the way finding the house more awesome in the morning sunlight. She could smell the toast as she loaded her blueprints and briefcase in the car. Going back into the kitchen, she caught a glimpse of the gardener in the backyard. She made a mental note they came on Tuesday mornings, as she did not want to be surprised again. Angie, the maid, spoke with Cassie while she ate and there was an immediate rapport between them. Angie seemed the independent type also, and she admired the fact Cassie was so important her company put her in such a nice home during her stay in Hawaii. Angie had met other executives who had leased the home, but they had all been men. She liked having a woman there for a change. As it turned out, the gardener, Joseph, was Angie's husband. The couple had worked for the homeowners for three years and thought a lot of them.

Cassandra thanked Angie for breakfast and excused herself. She went to brush her teeth one more time and then had to get underway. She was already feeling the butterflies. What if she got lost? What if she got to the facility and they did not know who she was? She laughed at herself. She had to quit putting herself through these question-and-answer games. At times, she felt like she put herself on such an edge that the gray hairs just had to be popping out.

Driving down the hill of the home, Cassie fell in love all over again. Every little detail on the property had been considered. Everything seemed to say that the owners knew how to enjoy and live life; not just pay the bills and go to work; but live, really live, and feel life. She wondered how some people were able to make that happen.

Following the map to the prison from the house that Todd had drawn up for her, Cassandra arrived without any problems. The biggest problem she had encountered was to stay on course and not do some sightseeing along the way. Everything appeared so fresh and clean in the morning sun.

After parking the car, she continued up to the entrance building of the institution. She was wondering if the team of men assigned to her by the company would be waiting in the lobby or if they had gone on in to the job site, or if they were even there yet. After all, she was early this morning. Again, Cassie had considered first impressions. She wanted the assigned team to be aware she considered promptness an attribute and she expected no less from them. Tight ship, got to run a tight ship, she thought. This particular job is very important to a lot of people for a lot of reasons.

As Cassandra approached the steps to the front entrance, she stopped to read a monument off to the right of the steps. After reading it, she could not help but wonder whose idea it was to place such a monument there. She liked what it said, but wasn't sure that it was appropriate, all things considered, for it was almost ironic. It read,

> *These are our gods, whom I worship;*
> *whether I do right or wrong,*
> *I do not know;*
> *but I follow my faith, which cannot*
> *be wicked, as it commands me*
> *never to do wrong.*

KAMEHAMEHA

Chapter 12

OSSING HER GOLDEN HAIR behind her shoulders and taking a deep breath, Cassandra put on her face of confidence and proceeded into the building. Approaching the guard at the desk in the lobby, Cassie noticed three men sitting on the left side of the room. The room was big, lined with straight back chairs and a tall ceiling with windows equally as tall. Even with the sun pouring in the windows, the room felt cold and stark. Cassie wondered if they were part of her company team.

After telling the guard who she was and stating her purpose in being there, the aloof guard waved toward the three men sitting in the lobby. He then stated that until the whole group was present, he wasn't going to contact anyone, so he wouldn't have to do it more than once. He then looked up at Cassie's face, and appeared slightly startled by the woman standing before him.

Cassandra immediately recognized the look and the attitude. At least seventy-five percent of the correctional officers at the Texas institution had the same attitude. They were in control and if you did not like the way they did their job, report them, they really did not care. It often appeared some staff received their promotions based on the number of complaints lodged against them. The greater the number of complaints, the better the promotion. As the officer continued to skeptically eye Cassandra, she thanked him and walked over to introduce herself to the three men already there. As she approached the men, she could read the doubt crossing their faces. She felt this job was going to be tough and she heard her inner voice saying, "Please, God, be with me on this one."

Smiling, she held her hand out, progressively shaking the hand of each man as she said, "Hello, my name is Cassandra Stevens and I understand you men are here for the same purpose as I." She knew by the expressions on their faces they were not only concerned about working in such an environment, but they were now doubting the abilities of their new supervisor as well. Cassie decided while they waited for the rest of the team to arrive she would discuss each man's capabilities, thus hoping to ease the tensions a little.

As the rest of the crew trickled in, and after the initial look of surprise at meeting Cassandra, each man quietly voiced an opinion of their treatment by the guard at the desk. Cassie told them they shouldn't expect the treatment to improve, that most likely the entire time of working at the facility they would all be under close scrutiny and suspicion. She told them it did not matter how extensive the background check was they each had passed, for the paranoia ran too deep in this particular environment. The men chuckled and asked her how she knew that and after telling them of her past work history with the State Bureau of Prisons, or the SBOP as they were called, each man seemed to have a greater sense of respect towards her.

The correctional officer made a phone call and then told the team someone would be there to take them to orientation shortly. Cassie explained to the men they would have to view some films, take a little test regarding what they had viewed, and a short discussion before they moved on to their workstation. She warned the men to heed the directions and warnings given, but they would find each situation encountered with the inmates was unique and would have to be handled as such; but to take their time and consider what might really be taking place and the possible consequences. She warned them to never do anything that might jeopardize everyone's safety or the reputation of the company.

The men started to joke around with each other and Cassandra felt they were starting to feel more confident. She had the ability to speak authoritatively, but with the sound of experience and understanding, never threatening.

In her earlier discussions with the men, Cassie felt she liked the older man named "Cotton" the best so far. His name fit, for he had cotton white hair and he was older and more relaxed than the other men. She chose to wait until she had seen him work to decide if he would make a good "lead" man for the team. "Cotton" had an easy smile and she detected a southern twang in his speech. Cassie feared she might rely too heavily on feeling comfortable with another Southerner, so she would reserve judgment until later.

An older man named Gibbs, the Prison Business Administrator, escorted the team to a conference room where they viewed a film, followed by short test and discussion; just as Cassie had said, nothing had changed. Afterwards they were taken across the compound by two guards and then led into the Captain's office.

The Captain was a very authoritative figure. He stood tall and lean, with a finely chiseled face, dark hair and eyes as blue as water. His name was Law, and while Cassandra mused herself with his name, she noted that he carried himself as though he had been in the military for several years. His uniform shirt and pants were starched and pressed, shoes polished, everything in its proper place. All business and straight to the point, Capt. Law called in the Lieutenant who was on the daytime shift for the current quarter. The team was informed that if they needed to do any evening or night work, it would have to be cleared by the Captain. Cassandra felt she could work with the Captain. He had strict guidelines, but you knew where he stood.

When she turned to meet the Lieutenant, she knew there was trouble. Lt. Applegris was a huge, overweight, smug individual who looked as though he had just come to the big city from the nearby hills. He took one look at Cassie and said, "Well now, this pretty little lady can't be a part of this operation. She might break a fingernail or something else equally tragic." Cassandra smiled, held her hand out to give a very firm handshake and with the strongest voice possible, "Hang around Lt. Applegris, you just might be surprised." He broke into a big grin and said, "Why thank you for the invitation, watching you work could be fun." Cassie wished Applegris had said nothing, and she no longer felt comfortable with a southern accent, on anyone.

Capt. Law brought the situation back around to reality making the comment that everyone had a lot of work to do and had best get underway. Lt. Applegris then escorted the team to the utilities room where the job would get started. With a quick smile towards Cassie, he said he would come by later to check on them and if she needed anything, anything at all, just holler. Cassandra wasn't sure if this was good or bad, only time would tell.

The men on the team had grown quiet and Cassie knew they were all questioning what it would be like working with the inmates and perhaps even wondering what they had gotten themselves into.

Cassandra moved about in the huge utilities room, pretending to look over the existing equipment. While she silently observed her team and the Lieutenant interacting together. Applegris was loud, and he had dark beady eyes, with a nervous twitch in the right eye. Unlike the Captain, his uniform was not well pressed, his shirt was too tight and his pants were too short. Cassie noted his thick black belt, heavy with keys, radios and other "toys" that the Lieutenant was obviously proud. His shirt was so tight, the buttons would hurt someone if they popped off. He was telling the men that even when he wasn't on duty, he was at the institution. Cassie found herself thinking that Lt. Applegris must have an exceptionally fascinating family and social life if he is always at the institution. "Stop it right now" she told herself, for this job is far too important to be developing such prejudicial attitudes. He would be an easy candidate to play mind games with, but intellectually, she knew it could also be dangerous. Everything, everything, would have to remain on the up and up, nothing but business.

At about the same moment, the guard arrived with the team of inmate workers. Applegris immediately began to set forth the rules to the inmates while telling Cassie's team these men were there to do the "grunt" work, any dirty work the company team didn't want to do. Any inmate caught not working for any length of time would go to "the hole". The dehumanizing game. Cassie recognized it right away for it started that same sick feeling in the pit of her stomach and she hated anyone who played it. Most of these prisoners were people who had committed wrongs against the government, such as not paying taxes, or hot check writers, lawyers who misused trusts, mainly people who had committed "paper crimes". They were not mass murderers, rapists and such. And they were still human beings. Cassandra had never seen the purpose in treating them as though they were subhuman. In her years with the S.B.O.P., she had never really seen any form of rehabilitation. Instead she had witnessed a great deal of degradation and humiliation, which only brought about tremendous feelings of bitterness and hatred from the inmates.

Cassie was saying a silent prayer for strength and patience as Lt. Applegris wheeled around towards her and said with a leering smile, "I'm sure you can get these prisoners to do any work for you that might cause you to break one of those pretty fingernails." Cassie smiled and said she was sure they would all get along just fine, and if everyone was through with orders and introductions, they had a job to do. Applegris, obviously agitated with Cassie cutting him off, turned and walked out of the room.

Pretending not to notice the Lieutenant's abrupt departure, Cassie made a move to get things underway. One of her younger team members, named Kevin, approached her and with a very pronounced mimic of the lieutenants eye twitch, he said "I think we can have some fun with that man, what do you think?" Cassandra chuckled and said, "I think we should do our job and not go looking for trouble." Kevin smiled and said, "Yes ma'am, let's do it."

Cassie smiled at Kevin. She liked his easy smile and laughter, and it seemed that he enjoyed mimicking and kidding around. Of all her team, Kevin was probably the youngest, certainly the most athletic and muscular. He towered over Cassie, and his hair was a little long, but neat and clean and his brown eyes danced when he spoke. He seemed prepared to be the entertainer for all of them, and right now Cassie felt they all needed to laugh and to break the ice, so she let Kevin run with it.

Without really being aware of what she was doing, Cassie was avoiding any real eye contact with the inmates. She made sure when she spoke to any of the men that her thoughts were in order and her voice in control, but she was avoiding eye contact and physical closeness. She told the men to talk with each other, figure out strengths and weaknesses. Decide who would work best together and she would work with whichever inmate was remaining. Cassie crossed the room, looking further at the existing equipment, silently observing the men, and looking more closely at the inmate team. Deep in her heart, she was certain she could still feel the pain she thought she'd left behind two years ago. Being here, in this institution, so close to these men, she could feel the hurt in her chest.

The remaining inmate walked towards Cassie and smiled a very soft smile as he introduced himself as Ben Brock from California. He apologized to Cassie as he stated she was apparently stuck with the inmate with the least of skills. In her easy-going manner, Cassandra assured him nothing she asked of him would take any great skills. While going over the necessary first steps, she found herself looking at Ben more and more. He had beautiful brown eyes that seemed to hang on to every word and since he was about the same height, she could look right into them. Cassie guessed that Ben was in his mid-40's and had most likely been a professional of some sort, for he did not possess the same physique as Kevin and his hands were soft when he shook her hand. Even still, Cassie would only guess at his background, she was determined to keep herself distant. Though she found his eyes alluring, she also found them intimidating. When Cassie spoke to Ben, she felt that he looked right into her soul, and she didn't particularly like the feeling.

Cassie retrieved a tablet and pen from her briefcase and instructed Ben to follow her and take notes for her as she analyzed the chattering repeaters and determined which could be removed first so as to not interrupt the communications system within the prison. For now, the constant chatter of the repeaters was deafening, so she wanted to remove them as quickly as possible. It was obvious the utilities room had become the "catch all" room, as it was full of junk that had no place in there. She then asked Kevin to have some of the inmate team help him move some of the tables where they could be utilized to lay out the blueprints and a desk area. Ben followed her closely taking notes as she looked over the existing equipment. Cassie found herself thinking she hadn't even checked his handwriting so she hoped she would be able to read the notes later.

Once the tables were in place and Kevin had Cassie's approval, Kevin laid out the blueprints for the work team to look over and Cassie joined them. Taking the tablet from Ben, she started to go over the notes with the men as to which pieces of equipment were being moved first and why. She then began reviewing the new configuration of the utilities room. Reading the notes, she was amazed at how nice Ben's handwriting actually was, and knew she would hand off the daily calendar entries to him. Unloading that detail would help her immensely. Looking at all the men, she told them one of the first things to be done was to empty out some of the clutter. She would speak with the Captain as to where it could all be relocated, then, out with the noisy repeaters. Perhaps then they could hear themselves when they spoke. Everyone nodded and chuckled in agreement.

Cassandra realized after working with Ben for only a short period of time he had a somewhat domineering personality and even though he professed not to know what he was doing, he wanted to be in charge. Whatever he did before prison, he must have been the boss, she thought. Figuring out how she was going to work with Ben was going to be a challenge in itself. There could only be one chief on this job and it certainly couldn't be an inmate. Somehow Cassandra would have to remind Ben of his position and for that, she wished she was working with someone else or he was not even on the team.

As Cassandra walked through the door of the house the first evening, she sat down in the closest chair to pull her shoes off, and just sat there, again admiring the beauty of the place. Barefoot, she wandered into the kitchen, opened the Sub Zero fridge and retrieved the bottle of white wine she had picked the night before. After pouring herself a glass, she looked out the window at the ocean beyond. Lost in her thoughts, Cassie meandered into the game room, rolled the cue ball across the pool table and watched it slowly drop into the corner pocket. The game room was over sized, and made for play. Besides the wet bar and pool table there were pinball machines, lots of seating and more ceiling to floor glass windows. The windows seemed to allow the outside beauty to flow inside. This was everyone's dream home. Being so tired, she actually considered laying across the pool table, so she kept moving.

Bathwater running, Cassie turned on the television in the bedroom, hoping to be able to at least catch some of the news. The news reports were all about how the police were hunting for a killer with some very unusual characteristics. The stories were alarming, but Cassie knew she had too much to do to give it much thought right now. She was so tired and there was still paperwork to be done. As she slid into the hot bubble bath, Cassie hoped that she would not be this tired every evening, or she would never get out to see the sights.

Cassandra slept wildly that night with dreams full of faces from the past. Faces that she had buried when she left her job at the prison. The next morning she could only recall parts of the dreams, but the faces flashed through her mind vividly. She wondered what it all meant. Was it to warn her, was it telling her to be more sympathetic and understanding, or was it her heart screaming out that she could not suppress what it had so candidly felt? For now, she knew she had to put it out of her head. With all the pressure she was under, the worries with her marriage, missing her kids, sleeping in a strange bed, it was all too much. It added up to nothing, just a lot of confusion and mixed emotions.

Chapter 13

RRIVING AT WHAT she considered to be early this morning, Cassandra found the inmate team waiting on her. She had forgotten. The majority of these men were well educated and full of drive. They hunger for something genuine to occupy their time and minds. For most of them, the hardest part of their sentence, is the boredom, the feeling of being worthless and warehoused. Cassandra knew by their early attendance the first morning they would all prove to be dependable, for they also knew, at the drop of a hat, they could be replaced and go back to doing some drudgery work.

Finally her regular team arrived, all feeling the frustration that goes along with the process of being allowed to "freely" enter these confines. All Cassie could tell them was to get used to it, for this is how it would be for the next several weeks. Kevin, the young team member, laughed and consoled the company team that at least they only had to put up with the system for a few weeks. All of the men laughed with him. Cassandra found herself unwillingly wondering what Kevin's background truly was, for he was a character.

As Cassie was pulling out one of her notebooks to look up a particular diagram, Ben Brock moved silently towards her. She felt someone approaching and as she glanced up, she found his dark brown eyes looking straight into her eyes. Momentarily Cassie was rattled, and she knew it was evident by her startled reaction. She laughed lightly and tried to pass it off with light-hearted questions about how Ben's morning had been. But she knew, by the sly smile, and the slight cock of his head, he was aware that he had touched a very sensitive part of her, that her wall of strength was not completely up yet this morning.

Just as Cassandra was regaining her composure from being startled, into the room burst Lt. Applegris. One of the inmates was watching the Lieutenant as he approached Cassandra. The Lieutenant caught the man watching him and hollered, "What are you looking at, Asshole?" The inmate quickly replied, "Nothing, Sir." Cotton immediately told the inmate to come with him to get some materials. Cassandra took note of Cotton's quick reaction, and his ability to pull the inmate away from the situation. Cotton's good, she thought.

Applegris gave Cassandra that same leering grin as he said "How are you this fine morning?" Ugh, Cassie thought, from mean and hateful to sugary sweet, his personality could flip in a heartbeat. She could tell already this man might be trouble. Applegris was about six foot tall, crew cut hair, plump with a belly severely inching over his belt, pretty rough around the edges. Cassandra found herself again looking at Applegris' thick black belt with the two radios, two sets of handcuffs, two long sets of keys, a key card and who knows what the rest of the stuff was. She wanted to ask why he liked everything in twos, but it was obvious he had hang-ups, so she decided to remain all business instead. Cassie smiled and replied she was just fine. The Lieutenant lingered for a couple of moments before finally asking her where she hailed from and then before she could even answer, what Cassandra dreaded hearing, "Well, some evening when you get bored, why don't you let me show you some of the sights of the island? Why, we could even do some afternoon snorkeling. I bet you look good in a bikini."

Cassandra wished she could just melt away, or better yet, make the Lieutenant forever disappear. Cassandra chose to ignore the offhanded compliment and thanked him for the sightseeing offer. She told the Lieutenant for now she had all time would permit doing her job and the paperwork that went with it. Applegris laughed a little and said, "Well, you just don't know what you're missing, little lady." As he turned to leave, Cassie could not hold back the thought that to spend time with the Lieutenant, she could wait a lifetime.

While walking out, the Lieutenant made sure to scream at the men that they had better stay moving all day or pay the consequences. Cassie knew with each rejection she gave the Lieutenant, her two teams of men would pay in some fashion, but she refused to be manipulated by his ill behavior. She put the thoughts of sexual harassment out of her head. Momentarily, the work room was crowded with a thick silence.

Cassandra turned to her laptop to check some dates and to make note of the behavior of the Lieutenant. One thing she knew for sure was to document every occurrence, good or bad. Cotton walked over and asked Cassie if they were going to have to put up with that man every day. Much to his dismay, Cassie replied they were, for the time being, playing on his field, and they had to follow the rules to the letter. Then she thanked him for his quick reactions with the inmate and told him that was a trait he would often put to practice in the current surroundings. Cotton smiled, then lowered his head and said, "Well, let's get this job under way so we can get through and get out of this place." Cassie laughed slightly and said, "My sentiments exactly."

As the day progressed, Cassandra found Ben to be a quick learner and told him so. She said she doubted even more what he said about knowing less than the other men to be true. Ben replied maybe he was pushing to learn more quickly so as to please his boss. Cassandra once again felt her face flush. She didn't want to feel what she was feeling at that very moment.

Chapter 14

O N THE WAY HOME a couple of days later, Cassandra was craving junk food. She drove to a convenience store she passed each day going to and from the prison. While paying for a street map and the local newspaper, she asked the clerk behind the counter where she might find a McDonald's Hamburgers or a Taco restaurant. The clerk pointed down the street and said, "Three traffic lights down and turn right, then go about three or four blocks, you'll see a McDonald's on the left." Cassie thanked him as she took her change from his hand. As she drove she pondered the difficulty stores and restaurants on the islands must encounter, not to mention the cost, in having supplies and materials shipped to them. As the voice on the other end of the speaker told her the total price of her burger, fries and drink, she knew she was right. The prices were outrageous. Tonight Cassie didn't care. She was going to go home, throw on some jeans or shorts, satisfy her junk food craving, and then take a walk on the beach behind the house.

For the first time since she got there she was going home before dusk and she wasn't even going to do paperwork tonight. For on this particular night she was going to sit down and read a local newspaper and study the street map to try and get her bearings. Cassandra longed to go sightseeing, but not with the Lieutenant. She was starting to feel comfortable with the home and with the job she was doing at the prison, and she needed more to keep her mind occupied. She did not want to think about her problems at home on the mainland and when she left the prison each day, she felt the need to mentally escape.

Learning her way around, to shop, see the sights, whatever, was a way to help her accomplish both.

The walk on the beach was exhilarating. Everywhere she looked it was a sight to behold. The bluest of waters, green tropical foliage, flowers of every imaginable color and sand that felt wonderful on Cassie's bare feet. She sat in the sand for a few minutes and took it all in, for this was another memory she wanted to hold on to for the rest of her life. Putting her tennis shoes back on after dusting the sand off of her feet, Cassie only hoped the walk would help to burn up some of the calories she had taken in tonight for she had really splurged, but she loved every bite of it.

As she climbed into the middle of the king size bed to read the newspaper she had bought at the convenience store, she could not help but read the headlines. It was the same story she had been hearing on the 10 o'clock news each night. Cassandra considered not reading the article; for she feared that she might stay awake listening to each and every sound in the house. She halfheartedly laughed at herself. She had heard bits and pieces of all of this on the news and it had not kept her awake, so why should reading about it be any different. "Honest to God, Cassandra, grow up", she told herself.

A short while later Cassandra realized that her first instincts were correct. To hear bits of the story on the local television news was one thing, but to read the gory details in the newspaper was quite another. Chill bumps were all over Cassie's arms. How could anyone do such horrible things to another living being? Whoever the perpetrator was, they were sick, beyond any kind of help. They were the kind that should be behind prison bars, not someone like Ben Brock. There, she did it, she let her mind wander off to Ben. He was an easy one to think about, she just wished she knew what he was about.

Cassandra decided that while her mind was on pleasant thoughts she would go take a quick bath and start winding down. Sitting in the bath, she began to do a mental check of the doors and windows and the alarm system. God, she wished she hadn't read that story in the paper.

After putting on one of her comfy gowns, Cassie climbed back into the bed, only this time she threw the sheets back and took the street map with her. She sat there quietly for a few minutes and wondered if she should do some paperwork instead. No, not tonight, tonight was to be a "forget about it night". Cassie smiled to herself as she thought of how she felt like a schoolgirl skipping class.

Startled, she sat straight up in bed. Cassandra had fallen asleep reading the street map. The crystal lamp by the bed was still on, the sheets still thrown back, and Cassie was wondering if the noise she had heard was just in a dream. But she did not remember dreaming. Either way, she turned the lamp off. She sat silently for a few moments with her hand near the alarm button. Her heart was still beating fast and hard in her chest. She could not believe the noise she heard was in a dream, she could not believe that would wake her up from a sound sleep. It was 2:10 in the morning. By 3:10 Cassie was starting to drift off again. She decided she must have been wrong, it must've been a dream after all. The remainder of the night was fitful sleep and Cassandra found herself awake before the alarm went off. Out loud she vowed not to read such newspaper articles again before bed.

Cotton and the other men ambled into the work room only to find Cassandra already there and working. Cotton poured himself a cup of coffee from the pot Cassie had brewed when she first arrived. The men politely spoke to Cassandra, then continued their conversation. Cassie went over to the coffee maker to refill her cup and one of the crew said, "Mrs. Stevens,

I sure hope you lock yourself up tight each night, cause with eyes as green as yours, this killer that's running loose, he might pick you next. After all, this island is smaller than some people think." Cotton turned and shot an angry look to the young man named Wayne, who had obviously spoken with little or no forethought.

Cassandra felt the rush of chills run up her spine as she bluntly stated she took great precautions as well as armed herself. She lied. Precautions yes, armed no. But perhaps that wasn't a bad idea. She quickly added she preferred they not discuss the homicides while there. She just didn't want to hear any more about it. Cassandra realized she was still scared from the night before. She took her coffee and went back to work. The men continued to look at her with disbelief. They never expected her to say she was armed, but they could tell by her voice, she meant business.

Slowly but surely Cotton got each of the crews working and made his way over to Cassandra. "Sorry about Wayne this morning, he talks without thinking." "No need to apologize for him, Cotton" Cassie said, "he was only trying to show concern for my safety and I appreciate him caring." Cotton stood there for a few moments, considering what and how to say what was on his mind. Finally he asked, "Do you really have a gun, Cassandra?" Without looking up, Cassie considered for the first time in twenty days of working with these men, that she really knew nothing about any of them. Now, with Cotton seemingly apologetic and genuinely concerned, she realized even he could be the killer. Cassandra turned to look at Cotton straight on and replied, "You bet I do, Cotton."

After lunch Ben singled Cassie out. "I'm concerned for your safety, Mrs. Stevens. I know you said you didn't want anyone to discuss the murders, but you do realize don't you, that this murderer has some kind of hang up. Just because we're on an island full of tourists does not mean a thing. This killer seeks out certain traits, the most predominant being beautiful, colorful eyes and you certainly have those. I'm not afraid to discuss this with you, as you know it cannot be me, for I am a prisoner here, and I do not think you would deny me my concern for your well being." Cassie wanted to throw her arms around Ben and tell him to hold her tight. She wanted to tell him of her fears last night. In truth, she knew her feelings were playing off of a need for an emotional connection with Dale right now, so she quickly checked her own emotions. "I'm okay, really, I do know how to take care of myself. But thank you, Ben, for your honest concern for my safety." Ben smiled, "Do you ever put your business side away and just be yourself?" "On occasion…" lightly laughing, "Thank you, Ben, really." Cassie said.

While driving home that evening Cassie suddenly took a wild turn to the right. The street sign was one that she had recognized from the map she had been looking over previously. Cassie recalled that about three cross streets down, if she turned right and continued on down, she would run into the ocean, and a very popular snorkeling beach. She pulled up to the beach, put the car in park, and got out. The water was breathtaking. The sun was shimmering gold as it began it's descent over the blue waters. She leaned against her car while she studied the beauty of what lay before her.

Walking towards the water it occurred to her that while here she should learn to scuba dive. Dale knew how to scuba and had even dove at this very beach on one of his trips here. Cassie thought maybe that was part of the problem, maybe she wasn't spontaneous enough, maybe she was too predictable. Maybe he had just grown bored of her. She made up her mind. When she got to the house she would call Todd and ask who he recommended on the island for scuba lessons. She would do something for herself, something spontaneous.

Driving home she was so proud for making such a decision to benefit herself that she wheeled into a taco stand and ordered the Mexican food she had been craving the last few days. Cassie concluded that she would go home, eat her tacos, take a good, fast walk on the beach behind the house, take a long bath and then give Todd a call at home.

Cassandra found herself humming to the music on the radio as she drove. For the first time in 3 1/2 weeks since she had gotten to Honolulu, she was feeling comfortable. The job at the prison was progressing well, the staff there was getting used to her and her teams coming and going, the men were all working well with her and each other.

She loved the house where she was staying. She was even driving around a little on her own and now she had made a decision to do something just for her. If her attitude and feelings about everything going on in her life continued on this course, she was going to ask Dale and the kids to come to Honolulu to visit with her. And if Dale had some inexcusable reason as to why it wasn't a good time, she would ask him to put the kids on a plane just the same. Cassie was determined that Dale copping out would not get her down. She knew that just seeing the kids would help her feelings.

Chapter 15

C ASSANDRA ATE HER TACOS and took a walk along the beach. Trying to work through some issues she had encountered with the blueprints at work, she was lost in thought. Letting the waves roll over her feet, tennis shoes in her hands, hair pulled back in a pony tail, she felt at ease, but knew she had to mentally work out the blueprints before she reported to work the next day. Looking out across the blue waters, all she could think was how beautiful it was here, Hawaii was a paradise. As far as she could see before her were the deep blue waters of the Pacific, and in every other direction were the lush green tropical plants along the beach. The air was salty and minced with the fragrance of the natural exotic flowers that grew all around. She marveled at the idea that her landlords felt the need to travel somewhere else for a vacation, to her, this setting was a vacation every day.

As she walked, she would stop and pick up a shell every now and then, and then carefully place it back on the beach as she had found it. Once while bending over to pick up a shell, Cassie thought she caught a glimpse of something moving in the trees behind her. At first she kind of laughed it off, thinking she was being silly, but the second time it happened, she became nervous. Cassie had traveled some distance down the beach since the first occurrence, but yet, there it was again. At that point she decided it was time to turn and head back for the house. She picked up the pace a little, telling herself she was probably mistaken, but to pay closer attention without letting her fears be noticeable.

As Cassandra walked, she had the sense someone was walking parallel to her in the tree line. She could feel the stare. She knew she had to get back to the safety of the house. There was no one else visible on the beach as far as she could see in any direction. Now she knew it was not her imagination, the last time she looked up into the tree line, she saw some of the tropical plants shaking as though someone had ducked into them. Cassie had the presence of mind to stay calm and controlled, so even though her first instinct was to bolt and run, she stood there, quietly reviewing the scenery all along the beach, as though she were taking a picture in her mind. In truth, she was looking for anything, anything that looked out of the norm, the print of a fabric, a shoe, hair blowing, anything that would validate the surging fear that had the hairs on the back of her neck standing at attention. Cassandra saw nothing, but she could feel the weight of their stare, she knew someone was there, someone was watching her. Casually she leaned over, picked up a small conch shell near her foot, looked it over and sat it back on the sand. Once again she began her brisk walk to the house, making it appear as though the faster pace of her walk was intentional. She could see in the distance the stairs leading from the beach back up to the house, the stairs that would lead her to the safe refuge of the home she rented.

Cassie knew when she reached those stairs she had to move quickly, cause whoever it was in the trees watching her, was further up from the beach and would have an opportunity to cut her off from the house. Once at the base of the stairs, she took off at a dead run, as though it was part of her work out regimen. She looked only straight ahead, completely focused on reaching the patio doors, keys already in her right hand, if necessary she would use them as a weapon to gouge her possible attacker. Reaching the door, Cassie carefully slid the key in the lock, turned it, felt the lock give, slid the key out and rolled in, quickly shutting and locking the door behind her. Not hesitating a second, she armed the alarm. Standing by the doors, she moved as though she were trying to cool down from her dead run up the stairs. All the while she was searching the trees and plants, looking for anything, rather anyone, for she knew someone was out there, someone who preferred observation to introduction. That someone scared her, the whole experience had just aged her. Methodically Cassie made her way through the house, closing all the drapes and blinds. Whoever it was would get no further opportunities for observation. She grabbed a flashlight on the table and went to sit in the gameroom while she quietly contemplated what she would do should someone attempt to break in the house. She knew that having a plan might help her in an emergency situation to move by instinct to save herself, rather than trying to make up a plan in a moment of extreme fear and confusion. The inmates at the previous facility she had worked at years earlier had taught her that because she had to cross a huge parking facility at the institution.

Sitting on the sofa, Cassie stayed very quiet, listening to every little noise and working out her plan, she had to have a plan. Cassandra woke up to the sound of the big front door being unlocked and opened. Jumping up from the sofa, she realized it was daylight. She had fallen asleep on the sofa, obviously tired from her frightening walk on the beach. Now frightened by a rude awakening, she scrambled to her feet, realizing what she had done and scared by who was coming in the door. It was Angie and her husband, Joseph. Tuesday was one of their days to come clean and landscape. They were just as startled to see Cassie standing there looking as though she had just fallen out of bed with her clothes on still.

Momentarily caught off balance, Cassie sat down on the sofa from which she had just risen and put her face in her hands.

"Oh, oh, I am so sorry you guys found me like this!" Angie asked if she was alright and Cassie nodded and said, "Yes." then she began to explain to each of them her experience from the evening before. Angie sat down beside her as she recounted the event and Joseph said he was going out to check the windows and see if he saw footprints in any of the flowerbeds by the house. Angie patted Cassie's hand, seeing how Cassie was visibly shaken as she told them her story. Angie picked up the flashlight and told Cassie she was going to cook her a decent breakfast and would have it ready when she got out of the shower.

Cassie showered and got ready quickly as she was starving this morning. Angie sat and had coffee with Cassie while she ate and Joseph came in to report he had found a cigarette butt, but didn't know if perhaps it had blown into the yard. Also, he had found what appeared to be a shoe print, but it was smooth, not like the sole of a tennis shoe, but rather a boot or dress shoe. "Had anyone come to visit who might have worn such shoes?", Joseph asked. "No, no one has even come to visit, no one other than herself, Angie and Joseph had been there since her first day there." Cassie responded. They all sat in silence for a few minutes. Joseph went on to say he saw no evidence of anything being tampered with, no doors or windows messed up, but they would call the police for her if she wanted to report and document the cigarette butt and shoe print. Cassie smiled and said, "No, it all seems pretty silly now, let's just leave it alone."

For the first time since Cassie had begun this project, she was late getting to the job site. And how lucky for her, outside Unit 12 stood Captain Law watching her walk across the compound. Oh well, she doesn't work for him, not directly, she thought. Walking into the workroom Cassie felt the quiet and she knew all eyes were on her. She had never been late, so she knew they were all wondering what was going on with her. As she looked around the room she smiled and said, "Okay, so I'm late, I'm human!" They all laughed a little and said their good mornings to her, and with that she tried to get her day underway.

After a bit she felt Ben moving towards her. She knew he didn't believe her little "jive" talk this morning. As he started his small talk, Cassie looked him right in the eyes and said, "You are so right, I didn't just oversleep, I didn't get caught in traffic and yes, there is a real reason I was late." Ben burst out laughing and everyone in the utilities work room turned to look. Cassie just laughed with him and looking at everyone said, "Do you all think it's funny that I am normal and simply had a bad start to my day?" Everyone just chuckled and went back to work.

Ben looked at her again and said in a deep and serious tone, "Care to talk about what's really going on?" After taking a deep breath, Cassie said, "It's nothing really, just me letting my imagination get the very best of me." "Like what?", Ben pressed. Finally, in a very brief synopsis, Cassie told him what had happened the night before, and then how the maid and landscaper had found her asleep in the game room this morning. She went on to tell Ben what the landscaper had found outside. As she spoke, she saw Ben's face getting even more serious. Calmly, she asked what he was thinking. Trying not to scare her even more, Ben asked whether or not she considered the possibility it could be the serial killer? Confirming she had considered it, Cassie suddenly felt sick. She had considered the murderer she had been reading about, but had convinced herself it was some silly jerk in the tree line the evening before. This put a new perspective on her situation, and just for a second, her fear was so great, she wasn't sure she could even return to the house.

At that moment Captain Law entered the room. As he looked around, from one inmate to the other, Cassandra moved around the blueprint table to approach him, he turned and walked out. She stood there, uncertain of what had just transpired, then she turned to look at Ben and he appeared to be as perplexed as she was, but he just shrugged his shoulders and said, "Let's get back to work."

Down the hall Cassie could hear Lt. Applegris yelling at an inmate in his usual foul way, and decided Ben was right, time to get to work. And for whatever the reason, the issues she had encountered with the blueprints the day before, were not an issue at all today. Cassie moved right along, she told herself to move forward, put the past into the past.

Chapter 16

THE YOUNG MAN had tried for a couple of hours to reach his girlfriend on the phone. Her name was Melissa and she and her roommate, Becky were supposed to meet him and his visiting cousin at a local club for drinks and then later, dinner at their house. Playing several games of pool with his cousin, he had not pushed the issue, but Melissa was not the kind to ignore the phone, nor was she the kind to not stay in touch when they had pending plans. Andy was excited to have his cousin there and he just knew Becky and his cousin were going to have a great time together. Finally he decide it was time to go to Melissa's house and find out what was happening.

No more waiting, Andy and his cousin, Ron, would just drive on over to the girl's little cottage and pick them up. If they weren't ready he and Ron would go pick up some beer for later and give them a little more time. By the time they got to the girl's cottage it was dusk and the house looked dark. Both girl's cars were in the carport, but the house was dark. Even Ron thought it was eerily quiet. As he knocked on the door, Andy felt the hair on the back of his neck begin to stand up and without warning, in this 85 degree weather, he shivered. Ron was already nervous at meeting Becky, and he could not help but laugh at Andy as he shivered and backed away from the front door. "Hey man, I'm the one whose nervous, what are you doing?"

Andy could only whisper, "Something's wrong." "What, what do you mean, how do you know? Hey, Andy, is this a joke or something?" asked Ron, feeling extremely confused. Ron was unaware of the recent murders on the island, but Andy was very aware and he had warned both Melissa and Becky to be extra careful. Andy started to run around the house to the back door and he yelled back at Ron to go next door, get the neighbors and call the police. Ron went, feeling really stupid, but he knew his cousin well enough to trust his instincts.

The back door was open, but Andy found that he did not have the courage to go in alone. He was afraid. Afraid of what he might be confronted with, afraid of the possibility someone might be waiting on the inside for him. He had even considered if something terrible had happened to the girls, he might mess things up for the police forensics. Ron came running around the corner of the house, finding Andy standing there stone cold, he approached his cousin carefully, sensing his fear, Ron softly said, "The police are on their way, Andy, just stay cool, there may be nothing wrong."

Andy slowly shook his head, "I hope so, Ron, but I've never felt this way before.

"I love Melissa so much, if something has happened to her, I don't know what I'll do. Oh my God, what if she's laying there hurt, possibly bleeding, let's go in Ron, we can't wait for the police!" "Wait, wait, the neighbors are coming this way, Andy, let's wait until they're here just in case there is someone waiting on the inside." Andy ran to the side of the house and saw the neighbors walking over. "Hurry, please hurry" Andy yelled at the neighbors. He and Ron took a quick look at each other and went inside.

Entering through the laundry room, they saw no signs of trouble, so they continued on to the kitchen. Immediately they were both set back by the dark, dried blood on the white kitchen tile. Andy could not decide which emotion was greater, his need to let his knees buckle under him or the need to rush and find his girlfriend, Melissa. Ron grabbed onto Andy's arm and said, "I don't know about this, Andy, maybe we better get out of here till the police come." "No, I have to find Melissa. I love her man, and I have to know if she's here!"

Blood was all over the cabinets and walls, the floor, the kitchen sink, and a trail of blood led into the living area. Ron followed Andy into the next room and they momentarily froze. Andy dropped to his knees and wept uncontrollably. Ron ran. He ran back out the way they had entered. All he could do was scream at the neighbors still standing outside the back door, "Don't go in there, call the police again, call the police, call the police, call, just get them here fast!" The woman reached for her phone and the man could do nothing but watch this young man he didn't know, crumble with fear and shock.

Minutes later the police drove up. They ran around to the back of the house where they saw the older man who lived next door standing. "Are you the one who called in?" and then they saw Ron on the ground, hunched over, sobbing with fear. "What's going on here!" the policeman said, his voice lifted to a higher, more demanding tone. The neighbor shook his head and said, "I'm not sure, his friend is inside, I don't know where the two girls are that lease this house." The policeman looked at his partner, radioed for their back up and then tried to reason with Ron.

All Ron would do is shake his head. Then he said, "Get Andy out of there!" With back-up on scene, the police set up their plan. With an officer at each doorway, the first two officers proceeded in the backdoor. They hesitated in the kitchen, both noting that the blood was dark and dried in some places, so whatever had taken place, had happened hours before. Then they heard Andy reciting the Lord's Prayer and they followed his voice into the living room. There the two policemen found Andy on his knees, his hands held in prayer, his eyes squeezed shut, his hands held close to his face. They looked beyond

Andy to the horror that had sent him to his knees, and both
wanted to drop to their knees as well.

There had been candles placed strategically around the
room and they had long since started to burn out. The two
girls, Melissa and Becky, were no longer alive, nor were their
bodies' whole. They were dressed, and Becky was in the floor
as though she were laying there watching television and
Melissa was seated in the rocking chair. Both of the women's
heads had been severed and placed on the coffee table with
candles lit all around them. Melissa's lovely sky blue eyes had
been removed as though a surgeon had performed surgery.
Becky's eyes were still intact, but reflected horrors unknown.
There was little blood in the living room which led the police
to believe the killing had been done in the kitchen. And by
the way everything was placed, the police felt the killer had
stayed there a while, he did not rush out immediately after
killing the two women. What kind of person could do this?
And why were Melissa's eyes removed and where are they
now? The two policemen helped the sobbing Andy up from
the floor and the three of them carefully made their way back
out the backdoor. There, they waited with Ron and the neighbors for the forensic team and coroner. No one had much to
say. Ron and Andy had stopped sobbing. The stillness was so
thick no one dared to speak.

The coroner ruled the murders had taken place around 7:30
the night before. It just so happened Andy was picking Ron
up at the airport at 7:38, so the police immediately ruled him
out as a suspect. The older couple next door said that they had
gone to bed right after the news and never heard a thing, nothing was out of the ordinary to them. The forensic team and the
police knew whoever the murderer was, they were in control
of their emotions. They had moved precisely and carefully, and
were not in a hurry.

Neither woman had been sexually assaulted, so it was not a sex crime, but definitely one of hate. To separate the head and brain from the body was to take away the control, it put the killer in complete control, and the killer had stayed around the house long enough to revel in his new found control. Money was still in each of the women's wallets and nothing appeared to be removed from the house. Nothing except Melissa's blue eyes.

Chapter 17

T HE STILLNESS of the tropical night was broken by the voices transmitting on two-way radios in the police cars parked all around the simple little house on the normally quiet street. Even though it was a street near the college and most of the little houses were rented by college students, it was generally quiet. Most of the students went to the beaches to party, they seldom partied in the close quarters of the houses.

Police detective Rick Parker came down the front steps of the little house and stepped around the corner. There, he began to throw up profusely. His partner, Detective Kyle Taylor, his eyes wet from tears he had quickly wiped away, waited on the steps for a few minutes, to give his partner the privacy and respect he deserved. Wiping his lips with his handkerchief Detective Parker came around the corner, his face ashen. Seeing his partner standing there, he knew he didn't need to make any excuses. It was obvious Detective Taylor was just as rattled as he was, only with a stronger stomach. They stood in silence for a few minutes, trying to get a handle on their thoughts and reactions to what they had just witnessed. "How could one human being do that to another?" Detective Parker finally asked. "I'm beginning to wonder if it even is another human." Detective Taylor replied.

Another unmarked police car rolled up in front of the house and the Chief got out. Approaching the two detectives, he read their faces, Chief Carson said, "Same kind?" "Yes sir, pretty horrific, too, so you better prepare yourself." The chief nodded, knowing he was not looking forward to going in the house. As he walked he asked the detectives if the forensic team and the coroner were still working the scene. Then he paused and said, "Once forensics are finished, I want that woman, the psychic, Hayes I think is her name, we need all the help we can get." Both detectives nodded in agreement, not that either of them had ever truly believed in psychics; right now they would try anything to put this crazed lunatic away.

When the psychic, Dee Hayes did arrive at the scene, she saw the faces of the officers standing around and knew she better prepare herself, this was not looking good. When she first entered the small wooden frame house, she didn't immediately see or feel anything, but as she progressed through the house with the police officer, the weight of the air, the smell of dried blood and open flesh began to overcome her. She stopped, collected herself and closed her eyes. The officer walking with her thought perhaps she was about to faint when he realized she was getting a sense of what may have taken place here the day before. The Chief entered the room and asked her what she thought. She hesitated and said, "I do not feel a connection, I do not think he was close to these girls." The Chief too, felt the suspect had to be a man, but he said nothing.

When the psychic realized it was both of the young girls heads placed on the coffee table, she gasped, but quickly recovered so as to not be asked to leave, and followed the Chief on into the kitchen. As she walked by the table, she saw the eyes were missing on one of the girls and cut out with a fine precision. She stopped and looked back at the girl's bodies which were carefully placed, one sitting in the rocking chair, and the other in the floor. Both deliberately posed, as though they were watching the television, and both were headless.

Once in the kitchen, seeing the blood spatter everywhere, she really thought she would be sick, but knew she could not cave in or the Chief would never call on her again. She slowly took in the room. Blood everywhere, then she looked back into the living room. The killer had taken them both in the kitchen, there was so much blood, she could absolutely feel their fear and pain and the overwhelming strength of their killer.

She surmised that Melissa was killed last, he saved her till he could have the time to carefully remove her eyes. The eyes held an unnatural attraction for him, but the psychic could not put her finger on what it was all about. She could only assume this man was very troubled, but seemingly took delight in removing Melissa's eyes.

At that moment, breathing in the thick foul air, she told the Chief that she saw a big man, strong and fairly well built. She felt he had met the girls at the supermarket, pointing out the bags of spoiled meat and produce still sitting on the kitchen counter.

The suspect apparently gave them a lift home because they had ridden their bikes, but then found they could not carry the bottled beer they had purchased, pointing to the 12 pack of bottled beer, on their bikes. She also pointed out that two bottles of the beer were gone, so they walked back into the living area and found the bottles of beer carefully placed by each body.

The Chief found the scene to be unsettling, as without a head, how were they to drink a beer? Both bottles of beer had been opened, but not drank from by the girls. Chief Carson felt a shiver go down his spine. Does this lunatic find this humorous, he wondered?

Ms. Hayes told the Chief she felt the man was wearing a uniform. A uniform that made the girls feel as though they had a new friend, and when he offered to load their bikes in his truck and give them a lift home, they were not afraid to accept. The Chief asked how she knew the suspect drove a truck, wondering if she truly was a visionary. She smiled, having seen the look on his face, and said she had seen the officers making molds of the big tire tracks in the dirt driveway.

She told the Chief he might need to be looking at his own people, she was sure the killer wore a uniform of trust. The Chief just stood there and looked at her. Ms. Hayes stood up straight, looked him square in the eye and said, "Chief, I can only go by what I see here and what I feel in this room, there is no one for me to talk to, to get a better feel, a better picture, to help with visuals. For this situation, I can only listen to what the rooms of this house are telling me, and what vibes I can still receive from the deceased, and I am telling you, the killer is someone they trusted, for whatever the reason.

"If you look at what is left of their faces, there is a sadness, almost like they are telling us they were so personally let down by the killer. He was not the person they thought he was when they let him in their home. I feel a huge strength in the room, the killer was powerful, and then there is the heavy air, sad, disappointment kind of air, and the fear is overwhelming in here. These girls last few hours on earth must have been horrific."

The Chief just dropped his head, then looked up, thanked her for her time and contribution to the case. The idea it could be a law enforcement officer was overwhelming to the Chief. In his heart, he knew there was something about the suspect that made the two young women trust him. At this point, he could not let any idea of the suspect get away from him.

Chapter 18

P ERHAPS SHE WOULD CALL Todd and see if he had any time free to go snorkeling or take her sightseeing as he had offered. Anyway, she could not wait to leave today, she was really feeling anxious. By the time she did leave the prison, it was too late for snorkeling, but maybe Todd would consider dinner somewhere. Time was running out and Cassie wanted to see some of the sights of Honolulu. The phone call to Todd proved fruitful and they agreed to meet at Wolf's Steak House on Kalakaua Avenue in the city. Todd had given her directions and had even offered to pick her up at the house, but Cassie declined, saying she wanted to learn her way, but truly, she felt her way kept the dinner more on a business level. There she was again, having to hold every situation to a certain level, mainly because she was a woman. Sometimes, she thought, life was just not fair.

Since Todd was still at his office when Cassie caught up with him, he was going to take longer to get ready. Having some time to kill and wanting desperately to "let the guards down" and talk to a real friend, Cassie decided to call a friend she had known since she was fifteen. He had been her first employer, and he had always been a close friend. The phone was ringing, and finally she heard his voice, the same laid back, fun loving voice was always a pleasure to hear, Cassie practically hollered into the phone, "Jay, Jay, it's me, Cassie, calling from Honolulu!" He laughed and said "Hey girl, how's it going out there? Sure have missed talking to you, even considered coming out there for a long weekend visit, what do you think?" "I would love it! Is Staci coming with you?" Oh Cassie, she thought, you asked about her too quick, Jay is going to sense your dislike of his live in girlfriend.

Staci was half his age, and as lazy as they came. Cassandra knew Staci was only using Jay till something better came along and she hated her for it. Jay had paid for Staci's education. She held a degree in Business from a major university, but had been unable to find employment of any kind for three years. Meanwhile, Jay had paid off her credit card debts, a ten thousand dollar loan she had from her grandmother, bought her a new home and Jeep Cherokee. He had taken her on trips any and everywhere and the woman didn't even seem happy. Cassie could not even stand to hear her voice when she answered Jay's phone at home. Jay was a professional, a very well known and respected professional in their area back home in Texas. Cassie was always amazed when Staci would answer his phone with, "Yeah?" Cassie longed to cut Staci down to size, but knew it was not her place. If Jay was happy, it was all that mattered, but Cassie hated seeing her friend being used by such a slob.

Cassie would run into Jay in the grocery store doing the shopping and she would ask where Staci was and Jay would say she was home watching sports on TV, and cover in some way by saying she was a home-body. Cassie would think to herself, "more like a lazy body."

Cassie loved Jay for the man he was, and she would never interfere with what made him happy. For if she was the type, she would have moved in on him years ago when she suspected he and Kelly, his ex wife, were having problems. Not only did Cassie have ultimate respect for Kelly, but she got the feeling the two had just grown apart. Cassie would never hurt two people who meant so much to her. Years later, she would wonder if Staci had not been in the picture prior to Jay and Kelly's divorce, for she knew Staci would never have such morals or principals. For that matter, even self respect and pride. Staci was nothing more than a user of others.

Jay kind of laughed, yes, he had heard the disdain in Cassie's question. "No, no, I seriously doubt it, she has a job now." Finally, Cassie thought. "Anyway, Jay continued, she's working for an airline, maybe she can line me up with a good fare over there, but she can't get any time off herself." "Well, that's a shame, but I'm glad to know it won't stop you from coming." Cassie said politely. "You're over there alone, am I right?" Jay asked. Cassie laughed and replied, "Completely, and I sure do miss the kids." "Well, I could load them up and bring them when I come if Dale will get them packed up and ready. What do you think?" Jay asked. "Ummmm, let me give that some thought. Okay, when do you think you could get here, Jay?" Cassie asked. Jay was quiet, Cassie could hear key strokes on his laptop, she knew he was checking his calendar. After a moment, Jay said, "How about this weekend?" Cassie was thrilled, she was going to see her friend much quicker than she thought. "Great, but as far as the kids go, I doubt I can make the arrangements for them so quickly, so just forget that, I'll get them out here in the next two weeks sometime. Oh, I'm so excited, Jay, I never anticipated this phone call being so rewarding!" Cassie exclaimed. "Me either, Cassie, I'm really glad you called." Jay replied.

Cassie heard something in his words and voice, but she could not pin-point it at this particular moment, for she was too filled with joy. "You can stay here with me, Jay, there's plenty of room." "No, no, thank you very much for offering, but I'm afraid of how that might affect your company. I mean, having your family come over and stay there while they visit is one thing, but friends start visiting, it might look bad. Besides, what would Dale say?" Cassie knew they were feeling each other out, and she knew he was right. "Oh, not to worry, but you're probably right. Well then, do you want me to make reservations for you somewhere nearby?" she asked. "Not necessary, just give me your address there and I'll make the arrangements, I know the island pretty well." Jay replied. Of course he did, Cassie thought, he had traveled quite extensively over the years. Cassandra gave Jay the address and told him she would pick him up at the airport, just let her know his flight schedule when he got it booked. Jay agreed and they both hung up after proclaiming their excitement to each other. Cassie hurried off to meet Todd for dinner with a new found happiness, and a smile that felt permanent.

Chapter 19

WORKING QUIETLY on her own, Cassandra was comparing some notes with her blueprints and her concentration was broken by the loud, arrogant voice of Lt. Applegris. He was yelling angrily and every now and then there would be a pounding on the wall. Cassie crossed the work room to close the door for it was obvious all the men working with her were disturbed by what they were hearing. Closing the door, she saw Applegris was pacing the hallway and was so red with anger he looked like a red balloon about to pop. One inmate was sitting on the floor in the hall while another was leaning against the wall. Beyond the three of them was the Captain. When Captain Law saw Cassandra standing in the doorway, he said nothing, he merely walked back into his office and out of sight.

Cassie quickly shut the door before Lt. Applegris had a chance to turn around to see what the Captain had been looking at before he stepped out of sight. With the door shut, she looked up to find the men in the utility room giving her silent applause. Cassie smiled, kind of shook her head and said "What in the world did they do to cause the Lieutenant to get so bent out of shape?" For a moment the men were silent. The inmate crew wanted to talk, to trust, but even after four weeks, they hesitated. Finally Kevin broke the silence in his usual joking manner, he said very simply "Seems there was a tour, big whigs, you know, who came to see the progress of the taxpayers money, and certain inmates who were handpicked to help with this tour, tried to slip some letters and petitions from the inmates to these big whigs. Anyway, it was observed by an officer who intercepted the papers, thus bringing about the Lieutenant's temper tantrum."

Suddenly the door flew open and Lt. Applegris, looking surprised to see Cassie standing beside the door, said "I thought it was made very clear to all of you this door was to remain open at all times!" Cassandra stood up straight and replied, "Oh, it was made very clear, and it has remained open for four weeks and it will continue to remain open. But when we cannot work for outside interference, if it means my shutting the door for a short period so that we can continue to progress, then so be it." The Lieutenant still frowning and looking straight at Cassie said "Well that's fine, but the show is over now and I want this door open!" Cassie nodded and said "No problem." As the Lieutenant started down the hallway, Cassie continued to stand there quietly. Looking out in the hall after the Lieutenant, she saw the Captain standing there again. The Lieutenant stopped to say something to him, probably to tell him what was exchanged between them, Cassie thought. Still the Captain said nothing to her, and again he walked back into his office, this time with the Lieutenant following.

Agitated by the exchange, Cassie found it difficult to tune into the blueprints. She found herself sitting there contemplating the two men in charge of this prison facility and realized they each had their own quirks. Applegris was loud, arrogant and incredibly chauvinistic, which indicated a level of ignorance. Captain Law was quiet, well mannered, carried himself with a strong sense of confidence, and the inmates appeared to respect him. With Applegris, you could tell the inmates had no respect for him. They were more irritated by his arrogance, but most were smart enough to avoid him, as he loved ruling by fear and threats. Cassie found it surprising the two men were able to work together, for personality wise, they were polar opposites, but then, maybe that was what made it work. No matter what, she was going to continue to keep her head down and get her job completed as quickly as possible.

Slowly, Ben made his way over to the table where Cassie was trying to read the latest set of blueprints. He began to make some notes in her laptop on the accomplishments of the day. Ben was meticulous with the notes and Cassie had come to depend on his daily entries. She looked over at him as he opened the book. He looked quickly at the other men and seeing that no one was watching, Ben smiled and winked. Cassie felt her heart jump. She knew Ben was trying to soothe her nerves, to comfort her after the exchange with Applegris. Without a second thought, she smiled and winked back. Ben never expected her response. For a brief moment, they just sat and stared at one another, each shocked by the other. Then they both broke into laughter.

The silence was broken by Kevin crossing the room towards them. As Kevin pretended to be putting tools away, he said, "You know Cassandra, I don't think I've ever seen anyone talk back to the Lieutenant like that since we've been here, at least not continue standing upright afterwards." Cassie was shocked. Was Kevin indirectly telling her the Lieutenant struck the inmates? She couldn't reply. Then she said, "What was in those papers the inmates were trying to pass to the officials on the tour and who were the officials?" There, she had probably asked more than she wanted to know. Kevin, seeming to have read her mind said, "Are you sure you want to know, cause I've been told a lot by the other team since we've been here working with them?" Cassie, realizing she was doing the same thing as in the past, getting involved, shook her head and said, "No, maybe not, just forget it, okay?" Appearing to be disappointed, Kevin said, "Sure, I understand." Feeling her heart sinking at the tone of Kevin's voice, Cassie began to remind herself that she had a job to do. She had to stay focused on completion.

Just four to six more weeks, Cassandra, so stay quiet and tend to your knitten' she told herself. Ben never looked up from the laptop. Cassie had always been amazed at the quiet respect most of these men conveyed to each other, even crossing teams, they had a network, a code, all their own. They knew who the snitches were, and had no problem with shutting them out or letting it be known who or what they were. Life on the inside was something these men would never really get over, unless they were habitual criminals, and those particular ones were hopeless before they ever came to prison.

It was almost time to call it a day, and Cassandra was ready. She wished she could take Ben and some of the others home with her. She could only imagine what fun this group might be in a normal setting, cooking out, relaxed and enjoying each others company.

Taking obsolete brackets from the utilities room to the storage room, Lt. Applegris watched intently as Cassie made her way down the long hallway. He loved the way she walked. Easy, confident with a long leggy stride. To him, Cassie was a spirited mare, and he thought he was just the right stud to break her.

Captain Law stepped out of the office to note what the Lieutenant was studying. When the Captain realized Applegris was watching Cassie, he immediately instructed Applegris to "get to work." Cassie heard them behind her and when she turned to look, Applegris was obediently following the Captain into the office. Looking past them, Cassie saw Ben and nodded, for they both knew Applegris had been leering. Cassie was glad the Captain caught him, and for a moment, lost herself in thoughts of what Dale would do if he caught Applegris staring at her the way he did. It made her smile, for she knew Dale would put him in his place.

Half an hour later, Cassie took her weekly report to the Business Office only to find Lt. Applegris sitting there by himself. It was Cassie's guess he was snooping, looking for any papers laying on the desks that might feed him some type of information he could share or use for himself later. She was grateful her report was in a sealed envelope. Applegris smiled and patted his lap, "Come sit with me for a spell." Cassandra put her envelope on the appropriate desk and walked on out of the office as though the Lieutenant was not even there. In her opinion, his crude behavior did not warrant a response from her. Thinking about Dale again, she knew he would flatten Applegris if he had any idea.

Chapter 20

JAY'S FLIGHT was scheduled to land at 1:50pm that Friday afternoon. Cassie had made arrangements to take off from work on Friday at noon and all day the following Monday. It was time for a few days of relaxation and fun with an old friend. Cassie could hardly contain her excitement.

The two teams at the prison knew she was taking some time off, but had no idea why. Cassie tried to keep her personal life to herself, but both teams of men made comments as to how she seemed to be walking on air. They all noticed a particular spring in her step. She just laughed them off and said she was finally going to see some sights on the islands.

She left the prison at noon, drove straight to the house to change and then on to the airport to pick up Jay. She decided to wear a denim skort, a skirt with built in shorts, and a red and white small checked shirt. She put on some leather wedge sandals, but threw some flip flops and tennis shoes along with a swim suit and a couple of beach towels in a small duffle bag. Putting the duffle bag in the trunk of the car she headed off to the airport. She was finally going to spend time with a close friend and see some beautiful sights. Almost five weeks on her own, she was ready for a change.

Jay came off the plane, spotted Cassie almost immediately and they rushed together in a huge, warm hug. Both were genuinely ready for some fun and good company. Jay loaded his bag into the car, asked Cassie if he could drive and they took off for his hotel. Once in his suite, Jay called room service and ordered a bottle of wine and some grilled pineapple. He then turned to Cassie, hugged her long and hard, and asked if she would mind waiting while he took a quick shower. "Of course not, I don't mind at all." she responded. Cassie remembered all too well how she felt after so many hours on the plane.

While she waited for the room service to arrive, she looked around the suite and noted all the little comforts added to the space, then decided to make herself comfortable in one of the chairs on the balcony. The bedroom was separate from the living area, so Cassie had no idea Jay was already out of the shower when the door knock came for room service. Rushing towards the door, Jay stepped out of the bedroom having heard the knock, too, and they collided in the hallway to the main door. Laughing, Jay hugged her up again and said how happy he was to be with her. They continued to laugh with each other while the room service was set up and Jay walked to the balcony to have a look outside. He was now dressed in khaki shorts and a collared polo shirt, sky blue, which made his blue eyes even more blue, and leather sandals.

Together they sat on the balcony enjoying the crisp Chardonnay and sweet, grilled pineapple. The view was breathtaking, blue waters as far as the eye could see with white sand beaches and palm trees that reached for the sky. The pool was on the other side of the hotel, so from where they were sitting, no pool noise, just a quiet ocean breeze and amazing scenery. Jay told her he had stayed at this hotel before, and watched some of the most glorious sunsets ever witnessed from this very balcony. Finishing the pineapple, Jay topped off their wine glasses and said "Let's finish this and take off, there is so much I want to share with you." Cassie agreed. Jay took her hand and they just sat there, enjoying life, together.

Preparing to leave the hotel, it was agreed they would do some sightseeing, go by the house where Cassie was staying, go to a nice restaurant for dinner and call it a day. Cassie knew Jay had to be tired from the trip.

Jay first drove her to one of his favorite beaches, then to a shop he knew she would love. After each had made their purchases, they decided it was time to start thinking about dinner. Going by Cassie's house, Jay was as stunned as she was with the setting and the beauty of the house. After walking him through the house they trekked down the stairs to the beach. Jay looked in each direction up and down the beach, then turned and looked back up at the house, then back at the ocean, and again back at the house. "Why would you ever want to leave?" was all he could say. Cassie laughed and said she totally agreed, living here was the life.

Saturday and Sunday were full days. They shopped, they went snorkeling, they took long walks on different beaches looking for sea shells, they had picnics, and shopped some more. It was all very relaxing and fun, and comfortable, they were comfortable in each others company.

When Monday rolled around they decided to go to the market and get some food to grill at the leased house and just have a leisurely day. As the sun dropped on the western horizon, Jay once again took Cassandra's hand and smiled at her. She asked him what was on his mind. His response was, "Just so very grateful, for my life, for my lifelong friend. I really needed this weekend, Cassie, thank you." This time Cassandra took his hand in hers, and they sat there on the patio for the next hour, chairs pushed together, arm in arm, feeling satisfied and happy, with life, with each other.

After an hour had passed, Cassie drove Jay back to his hotel. He would fly out early the next morning, back to Texas. They had said their goodbyes, and it was agreed he would have the hotel get him to the airport the next morning. They did not want their goodbyes witnessed by uncaring strangers. One last hug in the hotel drive, and Cassie returned to the house alone. She found herself humming as she drove. It had been a good visit, a sharing of good times with a good friend, and she would be forever grateful.

Chapter 21

I T WAS A BEAUTIFUL morning and the market by the beach was buzzing with customers. He knew she was watching him while he watched Cassie, and that would have to stop, he didn't need any witnesses. Quickly, he began to walk away, away from her, away from the idea or possible thought she may know what he was doing.

Suddenly, without warning, the woman began to move towards him, and as she got closer he realized he recognized her, which meant she knew him. Oh no, he did not need this now, she would spoil everything! Quickly he moved towards the tree line, she would have to follow him where no one else could see if she intended to speak to him. She did, she followed him! He could feel his temper rising. Have to think fast, come up with a plan, have an excuse ready. Find a smile. "Hey, how are you?" she hollered. He turned to face her straight on and said, "Oh hello, good, good, how are you?" he replied, even though he could care less how she was.

This woman worked with him and he had never cared for her, always thought her smile matched her personality, phony. She was tall, slender, medium build and long dirty blond hair. She carried herself as though she thought she was something special to look at, and truth was, she was ordinary, somewhat plain. There was a prominent hunch in her back, but she thought her long hair hid it from others eyes, but there were times when there was no denying she had a hunch back. And here she was, standing right in front of him, with her faded, poop brown eyes. He always thought when she spoke to others she was holding back her true personality. He felt she was a bitch, he had dealt with her type before. Momentarily sweet to strangers or acquaintances, but if you spent any length of time with her, she was mean and hateful, he knew her better than she knew herself. What he saw was a woman who thought she could push herself forward in her chosen career path, depending on whose back she could ride to get where she felt she belonged. He wasn't going to be part of her climb. She would never ride his back to get where she wanted to go.

She gave her phony laugh and said, "Do you even recognize me, I'm Julie, we work together?" He answered of course he knew her, and asked "Enjoying the day in the sun, too?" She again gave that same phony laugh, tilted her head slightly and said, "Yes, and you looked like you were enjoying the scenery around here, too." He maintained his smile and said, "Well, I thought I saw someone else I knew, but not sure if it's the same person or not, so I gave up." She continued her prodding with, "Well, you certainly did look long and hard to have not figured it out." she laughed again, but he did not.

Annoying, she is so damn annoying, was all he could think, but she answered his concerns, she had seen too much. Now, if something happened, she might bring his name up as a person who had been on the beach, and make him a person of interest. He could not afford to have that happen.

He continued with the small talk, then said, "I was just going to get something to drink, may I buy you something refreshing, too?" She laughed slyly and said, "I know a good little place just down the road here that makes excellent drinks, interested?" There it was, she liked him and was looking to use him.

Little did she know, he found her disgusting. He could not risk being seen with her, but now he could not just brush her off either. It was now or never. He walked a little further towards the clusters of palm trees, the sand getting deeper as he walked up the hill and into the tree line. Then he playfully said, "Well I might be, what else do they serve at this little place?" She giggled and hurried after him to catch up. She was so preoccupied with catching up, she failed to notice he was leading her away from the other people on the beach. Away from witnesses and people who could help her. Just as she got even with him, he turned towards her smiling and said, "Bitch, you got too close, your day is done. I have never liked you, you're phony like your boobs, with a streak of evil, and I understand evil, know it when I see it!" And with those words he reached up, threw her head back and slit her throat with a knife he had concealed in his belt. Her eyes were huge with surprise and shock. All that could be heard was the gurgling of her blood, and when he looked at her he said, "And I hate brown eyes, they're dull like you." With that he let her body drop to the ground, in seconds she was lifeless, gone. He kicked a little sand on her, threw some vines and greenery over her body and left the area. It would be weeks before her rotting, lifeless body would be discovered.

For Cassandra, it had been a beautiful day, full of sunshine, smiling faces and fragrant flowers. Sitting at the kitchen counter, she carefully unwrapped the native flowers she had just purchased at the street market. Laptop open, she was prepared to read up on each beautiful bud, as she wanted to know more about the natural beauty of the state of Hawaii.

Coming from Texas, she had never seen such natural, exotic foliage. The first was a plant that had intrigued her for years, but raising two kids, she had never taken the time to learn more about it. But here, she had time to spare, she was alone on a weekend, and she was determined to do some of the things she had been putting off.

The flower was called Anthurium Red, and she had first been introduced to it while working in the Marketing department at an amusement park in Texas. Along with the Anthurium she had collected cuts from the Ocean Blue Morning Glory which looked like there was a glistening star in the middle, the Hanging Lobster Claw, the Hibiscus, the Red Pineapple, the Rattlesnake Plant, named such because it looked like the rattles on a snake, but was a beautiful yellow, and then there was the Blue Butterfly Bush.

This was a weekend she had looked forward to, a weekend of educating herself more on her surroundings, learning something she could share with her family if they ever came to visit. She had spent the morning walking the street market by the beach, gathering the variety of flowers she wanted to know more about, and picking up some fresh pineapple and raw sugar to treat herself with later.

Tomorrow she might even take a drive that would take her further down the island into what was for her, unexplored territory. She was determined to learn and soak up as much of her new, temporary environment as possible. As she studied each plant, she carefully trimmed and placed them in a vase of water for enjoyment throughout the next week.

The days to come were full of work, but fortunately she had good teams of workers. Some days were nothing but pure focus, nose to the grindstone, and those were the days when she would go home, take a warm bath, eat a bowl of cereal and melt into bed. Those days were hard and exhaustive, but at least she would fall asleep.

Other days, there would be opportunities to talk or joke around with the workers and she would have fun and almost forget some of the people she was laughing with were inmates. When the work day was done, she wished she could take some of them to dinner so the laughter would continue, but of course that would never happen, it was just wishful thinking. But emotionally, after a fun day, it was difficult for her to wind down, she missed being with people and laughing freely, she missed having fun. So, when she had such days, she would have to take a drive, or go on home and go for a good walk on the beach to help wear herself down, in hopes of getting some sleep.

While Hawaii was a beautiful state, more beautiful than she ever imagined, it was just as lonely as any other state without family or loved ones nearby. She would have to learn how to entertain and occupy herself more, or the days and weeks to come would seem like an eternity.

She found she actually looked forward to Tuesday mornings at the house when Angie and Joseph would be there. They would share a wonderful breakfast that Angie had prepared, and it was the closest to family she had felt in a good while. Angie and Joseph were good people, and Angie kept her informed of island news and told her good places to check out and the best places to shop, depending on what she was shopping for that week. Cassandra felt like leaving them and this awesome house was going to be difficult, too bad she couldn't just transfer her family here and life continue. That would certainly be a dream come true.

Chapter 22

ARRANGEMENTS WERE IN PLACE for the kids to fly out for a visit, but Dale would not be coming with them. He said his own job was very demanding right now and he felt he had been neglectful of his job while she had been away. His time and attentions were split between the kids and work, and just did not feel now was the time for him to request time off for a vacation. Cassie found herself quietly smiling and saying to herself, as she was sure so many other working mothers would say to such a comment, "Welcome to my world, Mister, how the hell do you think I do it all?" She was glad he had gotten a taste of her daily life, but at the same time, she was extremely disappointed in him for not making the time, for the whole family. Screw the idea of ever having a honeymoon, she just wanted her whole family together, having fun.

The house maid, Angie, agreed to come in each day that week and stay with the kids until Cassie could slip away and spend the afternoon doing something adventurous with the kids. She had so enjoyed running around and sightseeing with Jay, and he had proven, as always, he was the best of friends, no strings, just a good friend. He had even confessed to her years earlier that as much as he loved her, he would never do anything to tear apart her married life, she would have to come to him if she wanted a change. Cassie found herself feeling lonely very shortly after he had left, so she quickly arranged for the kids to come out and have a great week with her.

The kids liked Angie. They slept late each morning and then Angie made them breakfast, and they entertained themselves playing pool or video games. Sometimes they would drag Angie down to play on the beach until Cassie could make it home. Angie had proven to be a good friend to Cassie and the kids, and Cassie felt she could never thank her enough.

One afternoon Cassie asked Angie to join them on their adventures and Angie showed them sights they would never have seen without a native Hawaiian. She shared with the kids their foods, their history and customs. They went to the Hilo Hattie outlet and Cassie let the kids pick out something for themselves and their dad. Then she had them each pick out a Hilo Hattie dress for Angie and a shirt for Joseph, Angie's husband. Angie was so surprised, she began to weep. She and Joseph had lost their only son years before in a diving accident. With him went their hopes for grandchildren. She hugged the kids for a long time and thanked them for sharing their youth, good manners, humor and stories of Texas with her. She said she had loved every minute and this particular afternoon was one she would never forget.

The kids each promised to stay in touch with her and Joseph, saying they would adopt them as their Hawaiian grandparents. Angie said nothing would please her more, and then she turned to Cassie and hugged her, too. And with the hug she told Cassie if she even considered paying her for this week of babysitting she would have a fit, for she had enjoyed the kids so much, she felt she should be paying Cassie for all the fun. The women hugged again and laughed away the tears, tears of joy and appreciation for the friendship they had developed. Cassie documented each day's events with the kids on film, and with each passing day, looking through the lens of the camera, she could see how quickly they were growing. Dale had no idea what he was missing out on, nor did he realize how evident it was to the kids that their mom missed him, they saw the loneliness in her eyes.

That Wednesday night the kids and Cassie had gone to bed early, as they were exhausted from the day's events with Angie. Cassie had allowed Leigh to sleep with her during the week and that particular night, even Shane had fallen asleep across the end of the bed. They had all been watching TV together and just fell asleep. It was around 2:00 in the morning when Cassie awoke to a noise outside. In the dark shadows of the house she made her way around peering outside for any sign of movement when suddenly Leigh cried out for her in the dark. Running back through the house, Cassie arrived at the bedroom door in time to find Leigh sitting straight up in the bed and Shane looking through the open drapes of the bedroom window. She quickly asked what they were doing and Leigh said she heard something and when she opened her eyes she thought she saw something move outside. Shane had run to the window to look out, but saw nothing. Cassie drew the drapes closed and sat on the bed.

Then both kids asked her where she had been. Cassie, not wanting them to be scared, passed it all off with having gotten up to get a drink, and didn't turn any lights on so she wouldn't wake them. Perhaps it was just her in the kitchen that Leigh had heard. With that, they all climbed back into the king size bed together, but Cassie didn't close her eyes again that night.

Chapter 23

C ASSIE HAD ONLY asked Todd to join them one afternoon to go snorkeling with her and the kids, as she did not want anyone in the company to know how much time she was actually spending with the kids during that week. After snorkeling, they all picnicked on the beach and Todd showed the kids some tricks for building sand castles. They had a great time with him, and Cassie thanked him over and over for taking the time to go with them. He said, and he meant it, it was his pleasure.

Todd offered to plan something else with them, but Cassie declined, saying she needed to look at sending the kids back home to Texas. Perhaps they would all visit Hawaii again soon and take him up on his offer. Todd was disappointed for his offer to be declined, for he had fun showing them around and being a kid with the kids, but he let it go. If Cassie changed her mind, she would let him know.

On Sunday it was time for the kids to return to Texas. Cassie could hardly contain herself. Putting the kids on that plane alone was one of the most difficult things she had ever done. She wanted so bad to go with them, or keep them here with her, but she knew it was not possible. She needed to get focused again and wrap this job up. Driving back to the house from the airport, she could not stop thinking of all the things that could go wrong on the flight back to Texas. Those were her babies, the only babies she would ever have, and she prayed every day to be able to watch them grow to be productive, caring people, and never to go before her. That was not the natural course, for a parent to lose a child, and it was a pain she hoped she would never have to experience. Poor Angie and Joseph, she thought. Her heart went out to Angie and Joseph as she recalled the pain she witnessed in Angie's eyes as she told the story of her son's death.

As soon as she arrived at the house, she called Dale to let him know the kids were on the plane and to verify their arrival time. She knew Dale would be there for the kids, for he had never been a neglectful father. She told him how much fun they had that week, and how very much she wished he had been there, too. For the first time, since long before she had left, he sounded sincere when he responded with sentiments of missing her and how he had repeatedly kicked himself during the week for not dropping everything and coming on out with the kids. Cassie felt her chest tighten and she thought she was going to burst out crying. These were words she had longed to hear. Maybe they would pull through this after all. As they were hanging up the phone, Dale told her he loved her and missed her, and she expressed the same to him, telling him she would be home soon.

Dale was a good man, with a good heart and a strong will. He had worked hard all of his life, and now, his wife was excelling in the business world, and he was learning to deal with her successes. There was no jealousy, just an adjustment period of getting used to others besides him and the kids needing her. Dale was well built, average height, taller than Cassie. Big strong shoulders, dark features, head full of black hair, and pretty hazel eyes. Both kids had beautiful eyes, too. Hard to tell though, if they had gotten them from their mom or their dad. At that moment, Dale's family was everything to him.

Dale had spent some time reflecting on their marriage while the kids were gone to Hawaii. He knew in his heart he was being neglectful towards Cassandra, and if he didn't come to grips real soon with why he was behaving this way, he was going to lose her, he knew he would. She was an exceptional wife and mother. She was true to everything she did and there was no reason other than his own immature behavior that had him avoiding her.

He knew when he married her she was intelligent and incredibly well rounded in everything she did, that was part of the reason he was so attracted to her. Then he smiled to himself, thinking, and it didn't hurt she was beautiful, too. Yes, he was a lucky man, and he knew it, but he needed to show it, he needed her to know he recognized her good qualities. He needed to let her know she mattered to him and he was grateful to be sharing this life with her and their kids. Dale would find a way to right this wrong, he had been selfish too long. He sat there alone, feeling truly alone, and cried. He would somehow show her he was the good man she chose for her husband, her partner in life. Dale knew Cassie deserved so much more.

Chapter 24

S ITTING THERE, quietly reading the report she had just written on her laptop, she heard a voice. It took her a few seconds to realize the voice was real. A male voice, softly saying, "It's okay, don't be afraid." She had been so intent on what she was reading, and had music playing in the background, she had not realized the sun had begun to fall, shadows were creeping into the house and the wind had begun to pick up.

At first she thought perhaps a television or radio was on in another room, so she carefully made her way around the house checking on things. The voice continued, repeating, "It's okay, don't be afraid." Afraid of what? Who's saying that? Where is the voice coming from? What was going on? As she entered the garage it struck her that she had gone out the walk thru door earlier when she got home, but did she lock the door as she came back in? She ran across the garage to the door, finding it ajar, and just as she reached for it, the door swung open with the wind!

Cassie had to grab to the outside of the door as it swung outwards from the house. As she grabbed around the edge to pull the door closed, she felt her hand swipe the palm of someone else's hand! She felt her gut tighten and her heart jumped into her throat. It took every bit of her consciousness to continue to pull the door shut and lock it without screaming and falling apart. As she bolted the door, she made a dash back across the garage to lock herself in the house.

Running through the door into the house, she threw the door shut and locked it, too. Standing there, inside the house, she saw the intercom and it hit her like a bolt of lightning! There is an intercom speaker in the garage, too! Whoever it was, whoever's hand she had just touched as she grabbed the walk through door, had been speaking to her on the intercom in the garage. Which could only mean he went out the garage door just ahead of her! She could have easily been grabbed by him in the garage! And for him to be talking to her on the intercom meant he had been watching her from outside and knew she was alone in the house.

Without a moments more hesitation, she hit the red panic button on the wall. The police would be there in minutes. She took a butcher knife from the drawer, backed into a corner and waited in the shadows for the arrival of law enforcement. It seemed like an eternity before she heard the sirens coming up the driveway.

The police searched for hours all around the inside and out-side of the house, but found nothing. Around the house there was so much foliage, footprints were nowhere to be found and dusting for fingerprints proved futile. Whoever it was, they were careful, so the police assumed it was someone trying to rob the house and had hoped to scare her away.

A police officer remained through the night outside the house. The next morning, after talking to Cassie as she pulled out of the garage for work, the officer left the location, too. Cassie didn't say anything to anyone at work, she didn't want everyone upset thinking she was the next victim of the eye murderer. Best to stay quiet for now, she thought.

Chapter 25

C ASSANDRA WAS HAPPY for Ben, she knew he did not belong in prison, and she could certainly feel how badly he longed to be with his children. At lunch time they all stayed in the work room to enjoy the chicken salad sandwiches and cookies Cassie had thoughtfully made the night before. And thoughtful was how she had come to feel towards all of these men, they were now her extended family. As they quickly and quietly ate the lunch Cassie had smuggled in, she silently choked on her sandwich as she wondered how she would handle the departure of the first one, the first one of course being Ben. He had looked after her, he had soundly consoled her when no one else noticed, he had learned her, he could read her face without her ever speaking a word. With him there, she had drawn from his strength, what would she do when he left? Cassandra, for the first time in her life knew the true meaning of being split down the middle.

She wanted Ben to have the freedom he so rightfully deserved, and to be safe at home with the ones he loved, but with him gone, who would she laugh with while completing this godforsaken job? "Get a grip." Cassie said to herself, before everyone else takes notice of her silence.

Cassie had witnessed inmates being released at the other institution she had worked for, but remembered the inmates always knowing ahead of time when they were to be released. For Ben, it was as though it had just occurred. This made the situation more difficult to understand, there was no preparation, no talk of what was coming, just suddenly, he was being released to return home to his family in California. In truth, it was none of her business, she was there to do a job, not to make long term friendships.

The day progressed as usual, and when it came time for everyone to begin to leave, Cassie found piddling little things to do so she would be the final outsider to leave. After a while she said she thought she would leave as well and she turned to Ben and said "How about walking me up to the front gate one last time?" Ben chuckled and said it would be his pleasure. For a short while they said nothing, each dealing with their own emotions. Finally, Ben said, "Cassandra, with all my heart, I want you to know you are very special to me, very special, and if you ever need me, for whatever reason, no matter how near or how far, all you have to do is call me, I'm never any further than a phone call away. I mean that Cassie."

Cassandra was fighting back the tears. She never wanted to hug someone so bad in her life, but she knew that behind these walls, she could not touch him. She managed to choke out the words, "Ditto that, you'll never know how much you've done for me or how much you mean to me." He smiled and said, "I think I do, but you mean even more to me."

Stopping at the gate, Cassie managed to look one last time into those beautiful brown eyes and said, "Good luck, I wish you every happiness possible in this life." Ben, knowing the guards were now within hearing distance and always watching, said "All I can say is, be safe, take care in all that you do, please hear and understand what I am saying." She smiled and they gave each other one last look and Cassie proceeded on through the heavy double doors.

She could not turn her keys and radio into the control desk fast enough. By the time she was seated in her car, the tears were coming so hard she could not make out the lines in the parking lot. As she drove away from that miserable hellhole of a prison, she sobbed out loud. It felt as though a part of her had been ripped out and she thought for sure the ache in her gut would never leave. How did she ever allow herself to become so attached to someone in such a short period of time and in such surroundings? The only explanation she could come up with, she and Ben just connected. They had become fast friends. She would have to count her blessings for the time they shared, but now, he was gone.

Chapter 26

T HE DAYS CAME and went, some more difficult, some more productive, at least there was some balance to it all. Cassie's mind continued to wander, thinking here she was, in one of the most beautiful places in the world, and all alone. No one to drive around and share adventures, no one to go to a nice restaurant and share a good dinner with, no one.

She had enjoyed the dinner she shared with Todd. He was a perfect gentleman, and after dinner had driven her around the island to see some of the sights he enjoyed. He owned a BMW convertible sports car and they had the top down while they drove. Cassie felt like she could get used to this lifestyle. Todd told her then how the rest of the staff at the corporate office were impressed with the work she was doing at the prison, saying that she was making them look good with staying on schedule and working the contract to the letter. She smiled, thinking to herself that was something she had hoped to hear.

Reminding herself of that now helped soothe her loneliness, and she would see this contract to fruition. For a moment she considered calling Todd for dinner again, but not wanting to interfere too much with his personal life, she decided against it.

There was something about just being alone and feeling lonely, and then actually being with someone, but still being lonely. Life, at times, no matter the setting, really sucked.

She worked on, missing Ben, having to do her own daily reports was a pain, and he had taken it on with no complaints, for her it was drudgery. Ben being gone may have been part of her feeling so down today. Realizing she needed to shake it off, she decided when she got home she would take a long walk on the beach, get some tacos at one of the food trucks along the beach, and maybe even have a cold beer with her tacos. The fresh ocean air would help her spirit, she knew it couldn't hurt.

Chapter 27

THE IDEA OF BEING caught and arrested was something he thought about periodically, but not something he feared. He could tolerate just about anything that came his way, for he had years of rehearsal of living a very difficult life of loneliness, loss and pain.

He never knew any family outside of his father and mother. His dad's parents had been killed in an auto accident when he was just a young boy, and killed along with them was his dad's younger brother. He felt that was part of the reason his dad was able to disconnect with him, he was afraid of loving someone and losing them, he knew the depth of the pain. His mother would never allow her family around him as a child, but he was never sure why. He knew her parents had tried to visit, as she was their only child, and he was their only grandchild, but his mother seemed to enjoy cutting them out of their lives.

He knew his mother had a mean streak a mile wide because he had been a victim of her meanness multitudes of times. Her meanness, her lack of emotion, the fact that when she looked at him, she seemed to look through him, it played a part in the shaping of his life, his mental attitude, his personality.

The fact his dad's affection was superficial, that he left him behind with a woman he knew was evil, to start a new family without him, at times, was intolerable. He was like poorly constructed pieces of Lego that was the man he had become. It was how he was built. He knew what he did, the way he lived, he knew it was all wrong, but he had given up a long time ago. The idea of being in a prison cell would be nothing new to him, he had been boxed up before, that too, had shaped him into who he was now.

Even as a child, he had considered how to get even with his mother. He knew he would grow up one day, and he would punish her for all the beatings, the neglect, the pretending, the emotional desertion, the humiliation, everything she had done to hurt him would one day come back to haunt her, he would find a way.

His dad, not much mattered about him, he had a new family. He was smart to get out when he did, but he should have taken responsibility for his only son, but was lame enough to think his money would take care of everything his son needed. The money could never buy what the boy really needed, and now it was too late to even consider it. The damage had long since been done.

When he was a small boy, his dad would take him to an ice cream parlor on his birthday, and they would sit and share ice cream and small talk. Direct questions regarding how the boy's home life was were never asked by his dad. Questions centered more on school, friends, maybe getting together to go to a ball game sometime, topical subjects, for his dad didn't really want to hear the truth. His dad's new wife never joined them, he was never invited to their home, and he never knew if that was because his mother would not let him or because the new wife didn't want him at their home.

His dad had a daughter with his new wife, the boy had a half sister, but had never gotten to meet her. It was as though he lived on another planet, completely separated from his father's life, and stuck in hell with his mother. On one of the ice cream outings for his eleventh birthday his dad had gotten some cash out of his wallet and went back up to the counter to buy some cookies to go with their ice cream. In his rush, he had left his wallet laying open on the table. The boy saw there were pictures in the wallet and quickly looked to see whose pictures his dad carried.

There was a picture of him when he was about four, riding a pony his dad had gotten him, which his mother had quickly sold and had removed. The other pictures, they were of his daughter and new wife. Family photos, real family photos, different occasions of them having fun together, something he had never seen of his family. What would it be like to be part of a happy family, the young boy wondered?

The very last picture he flipped to was one of his half sister, surrounded by other kids. His dad and new wife were sitting on each side of her while she blew out the candles of her birthday cake. A birthday party, something he had never had the pleasure of enjoying. Bunches of kids his age, with presents, all there together, with the mom and dad both smiling with pride, and the happy child between them. What was that like, the boy wondered? It came at him like a crack of frozen ice between the eyes. He would never be part of such a setting.

He quickly flipped his dad's wallet closed, jumped up and ran for the bathroom. When he was able to return to the table, his dad smiled and asked if he was okay, the little boy quickly responded with a negative shake of his head and told his dad he didn't feel well. With that his dad said he would take him on home, or to the doctor if necessary. For an instant the boy thought of saying he needed a doctor, just so he could have more time with his dad, but his heart was heavy, and at that moment, the little boy wasn't even sure he wanted to be with his dad. How many times had he let him down, left him behind and ignored his pleas? No, he just wanted to go home. Once there, he climbed the long dark stairs to his room. His mother was nowhere to be seen, probably drunk in her bedroom.

In his bedroom, he walked over to his closet, went inside pulling the closet door shut behind him. He took his dad's old shirt off the hanger, slid down the wall, and sat and bawled into the shirt. The shirt that had once meant comfort and security to him, was now just there to muffle his cries. He would never look at his dad the same, he had emotionally drained him over the years. And today, today was the icing on the cake. Icing on the birthday cake he had never had in all his years.

Chapter 28

ASSANDRA HAD SPENT a good portion of the afternoon sitting on the back patio reading. The sun, the ocean breeze, the sweet smell of the flowers all around her, it was intoxicating. Realizing she was getting sleepy, she decided to go for a walk on the beach. She had promised Leigh she would gather more sea shells for her and she had to hold true to that promise. Walking along the beach, she stepped in and out of the water, looking down and carrying her flip flops in her hand. Someone had left a plastic bag on the beach and Cassandra picked it up, thinking she could put any sea shells she might find in it.

Caught up in her hunt for shells, playing in the waves, she forgot for a while how lonely she was, and now looking up, she realized how far she had walked from the house. She turned and started back. She knew if she didn't pick up the pace going back, it could be dark before she made it to the house. Once the sun began to fall, it was gone as quickly as someone throwing an orange ball over the rooftop of the house, dropped to the other side in a flash.

She had found a few good shells for Leigh, but now she had to get home as quickly as possible. The whole time she had been there, Cassie had made it a point to be inside the house before dark, unless she was in her car, which she just drove into the garage and everything locked behind her. Other people were still on the beach, but it did not matter to her, she needed to get home. It was the idea of being in that big home alone, and approaching it in the dark by herself really scared her.

Suddenly there was a man walking by her and she looked over at him, as he did her, and it hit her, she knew this man. He slowed down and laughed and said, "Hello". Cassie laughed and said, "Wow, I did not recognize you in street clothes, I'm so used to seeing your uniform." They both laughed and he made a comment about how it did make a difference in how people appeared. Then he went on to ask her how she came to be on that particular beach and she said she was staying in a rental home nearby and was just out collecting some shells for her daughter.

She then proceeded to ask why he was on that same beach, did he live nearby, too? His response was simple, he came out there to run, walk, whatever he felt like that day. He personally thought this beach was one of the prettiest on the island, and it was how he cleared his head. Cassie said she understood, and she hated to rush off, but needed to get on back. He politely offered to walk with her since his car was located at the park just down from where she was living. Cassie was glad to have the company, it relieved some of her fears.

As they approached the stairs leading up to the rental, Cassie stopped and asked him how much further was his car? His response was a casual, just a mile or so, and he would run that last mile to make up for having walked with her. They both laughed again, and Cassie thought to herself how nice it was to have simple conversation with him as they had never really talked to each other much before.

Looking up towards the house, he offered to walk up with her saying it would be just as quick to run to his car from the street side as on the beach. Cassandra said that would be great, she would appreciate the company. As they walked the stairs he pointed out the different plants along the way, and having studied up on the local foliage, she was able to contribute to some of what he was telling her. He commented that he was impressed she had taken such interest in her new surroundings. At the patio, he stopped and turned to look back at the beach and said, "Wow, I could get used to a view like this." Cassie could not help but smile, for that was almost the same thought she had had earlier.

Standing there, she suddenly had an urge to offer him a glass of iced tea, she didn't want to seem rude or unsocial. She had no reason not to trust him. He said he would love a glass of tea, and he would just continue to enjoy the view of the beach while she went inside to get it. Cassie smiled and said she would be right back.

She sat her flip flops by the door as she went in so as to not track beach sand in the house. Once inside she sat the bag with Leigh's sea shells on the counter as she went around to the refrigerator for the tea. Sitting the tea pitcher on the bar she turned back to the cabinet to get two glasses and as she turned to get ice, there he was, standing right by the refrigerator watching her. She tried to stay calm, but it rattled her. He had come into the house without an invitation, and he had said he would continue to enjoy the view outside. What was going on here, she thought anxiously?

Without warning he took the two glasses from her hands and said "Here, let me help." Cassie, still shaken and trying to hide it, just gave a simple nod and said, "Thanks." She turned towards the tea pitcher while he filled the glasses with ice from the front of the fridge. Unknowingly, she found herself looking for the emergency button in the kitchen. She could not remember if she had ever seen one in the kitchen! Then it hit her, it was by the door going to the garage, just past the laundry room.

Cassie turned back to him and said, "If you don't mind pouring our tea and taking it out to the patio for us, I need to change out some laundry real quick and then I'll be right out." The man knew what she was doing, for he had been there before when she had pushed that very same panic button, but tonight he did not intend to give her the chance. He just smiled and said that sounded good, but as she turned to walk towards the laundry room, he sat the tea pitcher down and went after her.

She heard him coming and took off at a run, but he was on her before she knew it! Now all she could think of was how to save herself. She turned and punched him square in the face, then kicked right into his crotch. He was momentarily stunned and she again turned and ran.

This time she made it to the emergency button but he tackled her right after she pushed it. He had his arms around her in a tight grip and she could not free her arms. He carried her back into the kitchen where he began to tell her how it would all be over before she knew it, he had waited a long time for this and now, now it was happening.

Cassie spit, she kicked, she did everything she could manage, but to no avail. He threw her face down on the floor and sat on her back. Then he pulled a roll of duct tape out of the pocket of his cargo shorts and while holding her two hands in just one of his, he wrapped the duct tape around her wrists so tight it was cutting into her skin. Cassie continued to kick, even though he was behind her, then she began to scream as loud as she could. He laughed and asked her who in the world was going to hear her, there was no one around for a mile?

Cassie informed him she had pushed the emergency button, the police would be there very soon. Again he laughed and leaned over her back and said "I will be through with you and long gone before they ever arrive, this isn't my first rodeo here. I know how long the response time is to get to this location!"

Cassandra began to plead with him, "Why, why are you doing this to me, Captain Law?" He stood her up and turned her towards him. He looked down into her eyes and said, "I need your beautiful green eyes for my collection. I have such a wonderful collection of jewels, and your eyes will finish my collection. What a beautiful gift it will make." He seemed to be lost in a trance as he spoke of his collection. Cassie took advantage of the moment and again, squarely punched a knee into his crotch. She was not going to go down this way, she had kids who needed her, she was not going to be a part of his sick collection!

Knowing she could not unlock and open the door with her hands tied behind her back, she ran for the patio door. It had to still be open from when he came in the house or she would have heard when he closed it. Running around the counter, she realized she was barefoot, but that was not going to stop her now. She got to the patio door and ran right outside, making a quick cut to the left towards the front of the house. She knew to run towards the road, not the beach, she wanted to be going in the direction she knew the police would be coming, or perhaps even a car on the road.

Just as she ran past the side of the house, she heard the front door open and out he came, running full bore after her. Cassie ran even harder! She knew her life was now in her hands and she was not giving up, she would live to see her kids and husband again no matter what. She could hear him gaining on her, his feet hitting the ground hard as he ran to catch up. Sweat was flying into her eyes from her forehead. She had to keep blinking so she could see where she was running. Hearing his feet pounding the ground behind her was deafening!

Then he began to yell after her and say, "Don't be afraid, it will all be over very soon, don't be afraid." Cassandra then knew, it had been him in the garage, when she had pushed the emergency button before! He had come for her then, it was his voice on the intercom telling her not to be afraid! That was how he knew what the response time for the police would be!

For an instant she felt sick, almost slowing down and giving up. He had put a lot of planning into killing her. He was sick! With that in mind, she ran as hard as she could!

Cassie began to scream, "HELP!", but found it difficult to yell and run for her life at the same time. She heard him laughing behind her as he said, "Scream, scream! No one will ever hear you!" His confidence scared her, but she could not let him win!

There! There were the sirens, the police were coming! Keep going Cassie, you're going to make it, she told herself! He took a chance and leaped for her, thinking if he could grab her now, he could drag her off into the foliage and palm trees before the police hit the driveway. Then the police would just find an empty house and most likely go down to check the beach area first. He would then drag her through the foliage to where his car was parked. He had a mission, he had to complete his collection, it was a very important gift, he had to make it happen.

As he leaped for her, Cassie glanced back and darted to the right, causing him to hit her off center, but he still knocked her to the ground. Getting up was difficult with her hands bound behind her back, and now her mouth was full of dirt, too. She scrambled and got up before him, but he was on her again, breathing hard in her right ear, and without even thinking, Cassie threw her head back and head butted him. She then jumped to run again, but he grabbed her ankle and they struggled around on the ground for a minute or so, and then the headlights of the police cars lit them up as they turned down the driveway. Cassie knew it was not over, she was prepared to continue to fight, but Captain Law got up and ran into the thick foliage.

One officer jumped from the car with gun drawn, and ran to Cassie while the other officer radioed for more units. Once up off the ground and duct tape cut away from her wrists, Cassie began to yell at the police to get another unit to the public parking area on down the road as that is where he said he parked his car. She told them he was the serial killer they had been looking for, he came to take her eyes for his collection.

Then she told them who he was, and both officers seemed to be in disbelief, for they knew him too, they had worked with him on different occasions. The officers put Cassie in the car and they drove down to the house. Once there, Cassie ran inside with the officers close behind. She told them to lock the door and she ran to the patio door to close and lock it, too. The officers instructed Cassie not to touch anything more till the Crime Scene Investigation team arrived. Cassie looked at them and said, "I won't touch anything so long as you are constantly touching your guns!" The officers nodded in agreement, they were shook up, too. They had all been trying to capture this killer for months, and each of them had seen some of his handy work, they knew what he was capable of and it was horrific.

A voice came across the radio, it was the other police unit that had been directed to the park. The officers were there, but no sign of anyone, a few cars in the parking lot, but no people. The responding officer told the park officer on the radio who the suspect was and what he had attempted to do to Cassie. More units were dispatched to comb the area. The officers in the public parking lot were checking license plates on each vehicle parked there, and sure enough, a Chevy Tahoe there was registered to Captain Timothy Law.

It was for real, he was the killer they had been searching for, much to all their disbelief. One officer was watching out a front window as another police unit pulled up to the house. He opened the door and let them in, but he quickly locked the door behind them. The killer was still on the loose, and no one wanted to test just what he was capable of, or how far he would go, especially knowing his background and the weapons he had access to at anytime.

Chapter 29

C ASSANDRA SAT ALONE on the sofa, trying desperately to muffle her fearful sobbing, when she heard a familiar voice, "I told you that if you ever needed me, all you had to do was call, so why didn't you?" she heard his voice say. For a moment she thought perhaps she was experiencing a hysterical delusion and then she looked up, straight up into those brown eyes she had grown so fond of inside the prison. She couldn't speak. She simply held her arms up to him. Ben sat down beside her, wrapped his arms around her quivering body and held her while she cried. Through her tears she said she didn't feel right calling him in California with a situation she was having in Hawaii, just like calling Dale, too many miles. She had to depend on local law enforcement to help, not either of them, an ocean away.

After a short while, Detectives Parker and Taylor came into the living room and approached Ben and Cassandra. "Well you sure knew what you were talking about Ben. Perhaps if the brass had listened to your hunches earlier, maybe we could have stopped him sooner, but no one wanted to believe it could be true." said Detective Parker. "I would like to be the first to shake your hand and commend you for all you endured to stay with your instincts to stop this beast. Congratulations on a job well done, Detective Brock", said Detective Taylor. "Oh yes, Congratulations." said Detective Parker. By now, Cassandra had stopped crying, but she still couldn't find the words to speak. Ben hugged her close and quietly said, "As soon as the police get through, would you like me to take you somewhere else for the night so you can feel safe?" Cassie looked at him and said "Can you stay with me tonight?" Ben kissed her forehead and said, "I wouldn't leave you alone for anything tonight. I'll stay with you for as long as you need me and for as long as I can." Cassie began to softly cry, her strength in Hawaii had returned, and he was now holding her in his arms.

As the police and forensic team cleared out, the Chief came over to Ben and shook his hand. The Chief said "I hate to think how much longer this could have gone on had you not done what you do best. Thank you, Detective Brock." Then the Chief looked at Cassandra and said the city of Honolulu would be happy to put her up in a safe hotel for the remainder of her stay, if it would make her feel better. Cassie thanked the Chief and said at that very moment she did not know what she wanted to do, but if she did indeed go to a hotel, her company would pick up the tab.

Then Cassandra looked straight at the Chief and thanked him and his men for being so quick to respond, otherwise there could have been a different outcome to her days events. The Chief nodded, for he knew exactly what Cassandra was referring to, but then he told her, "The person she really needed to thank was Detective Brock, for he was the one who had mapped it all out for his department. And he told us, without a doubt, he knew you were the next victim, so with or without us, he was coming out here to your house. We decided to take a chance, what did we have to lose, we have grasped at straws the entire time. So when your alarm call for help came in to dispatch, we were already half way here. Detective Brock is an intelligent and caring man of the law and you are lucky that he is. I am proud to be a part of the same team with him." The Chief again shook Ben's hand and touched Cassie's shoulder and said, "If we can be of any service, in any way, please, please call us." Cassie thanked him and the Chief moved into the kitchen with the rest of his men. Then they received word the killer was dead. The Chief informed Cassie, and said if she was staying at the house, he was going to leave a unit over night to watch the house, just for safety.

It was then she realized Ben had never left the island, he had not returned to California as she had thought. Finally Cassandra said, "So,... you're really a detective? Why didn't you ever tell me?" Ben smiled, "You never asked, and you know I couldn't. Now tell me, do you want to leave or do you feel safe enough to stay here tonight?" "With you, I feel safe anywhere." she said. Her response made him smile and he held her close for a few minutes just to reassure her she was safe now.

As the police chief stood over Cassandra, he was telling her that her husband had been contacted and he was flying out tonight to be with her, there was just no fast way to get him there. It all seemed to be a blur, but she nodded to the Chief as though she understood. Ben took her hand in his, and told her he would stay with her until Dale arrived, she would not be left alone. Again, she nodded, still in a blur.

The Chief began talking with Ben, telling him how he could not believe a man who had so much going for him, and appeared to all who knew him, to be a decent person, was responsible for the murders. Ben stated that when he began to look into the Captain's background, things just didn't add up, then when he looked into his living situation here on the island, it was strange; he was always alone, no one to answer to but himself.

Then when he heard the report from the Physic, stating she felt the suspect was someone in uniform. He began to document the Captain much more carefully, then it began to add up for him. He knew his suspicions were correct. He had watched how the Captain watched Cassandra, and felt it was just a matter of time.

Hearing her name, Cassie looked at Ben and said, "What, what did you just say? You saw him watching me? When, where, how did I miss seeing him watch me?" She was shocked to hear this information, as she felt she was aware of everything at the prison. Ben smiled, explained there were several times when she would have him writing reports, and she would be working with Kevin or Cotton and the Captain would slip into the utility room and observe. He said at first he thought the Captain was just being certain they were all working, but realized after a while he was stone cold focused on Cassandra, and he knew he had to get released from the prison quickly. It was then the Chief left to go to Captain Law's residence, said he had to see it for himself.

Cassie shook her head and stated she was aware when Applegris came into the utilities room, how did she miss the Captain? Ben told her Applegris always came in huffing and puffing, everyone knew when he arrived. Captain Law moved very quietly, almost in stealth mode, like a hunter going after his prey, so Ben felt he had to watch him even more closely. The Captain was well trained to be a killer, and he blended well as law enforcement. The Captain was obsessive, very regimented, and checked every detail. He was a very dangerous combination and he used it all to his advantage. Cassie could not believe she had been so blind, but then she was there to do a job, not to capture a killer.

Chapter 30

B EN CONCLUDED there were no broken windows or doors, the alarm system was still functioning and all her clothes and necessities were there, but if it would make her feel better, he would take her to a hotel. Cassie smiled, "just stay with me, that's all I need." Ben stood up and then he took her hands and pulled her up from the sofa. He told her to lead the way to the bedroom. There, she sat on the corner of the bed while Ben walked over to the dresser and began to open the drawers. Finding the drawer with her nightclothes, he picked out a gown, nothing revealing, soft blue and simple with a robe to match. Cassandra could only watch, for she was still rattled over the evening's events, and shocked she was even sitting in the bedroom with Ben Brock.

Ben, carrying the nightgown and robe, took Cassie by the hand and led her to the bathroom. He went over to the big bath Cassandra had fallen in love with and started the water to fill it up. He looked through the array of bath beads and bubble baths and chose the peach scented bubble bath, the very one she had chosen her first night in this house. One by one he lit the abundance of candles Cassandra had collected and placed in the bathroom.

Ben then walked over to Cassandra, reached up under her camp shirt and first unbuttoned and then unzipped her shorts. One slight tug and the shorts fell to the floor. Ben said "Step out of them." She did. Then one by one, he undid the buttons on her shirt. Cassie was nervous, but she did not stop him. Ben stood there for a moment, a facing of her shirt in each of his hands, he looked Cassandra in the eyes, let go of her shirt, reached around her back and gently released her bra. They both stood there, not daring to even breathe, and then Ben turned away to check the water temperature running in the bath and at the same time he added some more bubbles.

He turned back to Cassie, who was still standing there in her own lost way. She had never said a word. Ben put his hands inside her shirt and held her waist. He said "Slip off your clothes, get in the bath, and I'll be right back." For a moment Cassie felt a surge of fear and she said, "Don't leave me!" Ben hugged her and whispered, "I'll be right back, get undressed and get in the warm bath." As Ben walked out, he flipped off the light switch and turned to look at Cassie in the glow of the candlelight. He smiled softly and walked out. Cassandra removed what was remaining of her clothes and dropped them on top of her shorts on the floor. She then twirled her long hair up like a french twist and put a clip in to hold it on top of her head.

She slipped into the warm bath and decided the tub was full enough. The bubbles came just to her shoulders, covering her bare breasts. She laid back and closed her eyes. The tears began to silently flow from the outer corners of her eyes as she thought of how different this evening could have turned out. It was then that she felt Ben sitting on the side of the bath. She opened her eyes as he took a dry washcloth to wipe away her tears. Cassandra smiled and said how blessed she felt to have him there with her. Ben wet the washcloth and put a little soap on it and began to wash the dirt from her face. Cassie felt like a child. She could not remember the last time anyone had soaped a washcloth and bathed her. But she wasn't going to fight it.

Tonight there would be no show of a modern woman, no facade of womanly strength, tonight she would be nothing more than putty in Ben's hands. He handed Cassie a chilled glass of Chardonnay and told her to lean forward so he could wash her back. Cassie realized Ben had done everything as she had liked it, the peach bubble bath, the candles, the white wine, everything. She had never told him, for at the prison there had never even been such talk. Either he knew her better than she thought or they shared common pleasures. She smiled to herself, for whichever it was, she loved it. As Ben washed her back, he told her there would be no more talk tonight of the prison, why he was a detective, or even how he put it all together. Tonight it would only be the two of them, the talk or the silence, would only be of the two of them.

Ben added hot water to keep the bath warm, then he took the wine glass from Cassie's hand and put it to the side. He pulled her close to the edge of the bath and wrapped his arms around her soft naked body and said, "Do you recall one evening as you were leaving and you had been having trouble sleeping for several nights?" Cassie managed to murmur an "uh-huh." Ben continued with, "as you reached the front gate I said, now go home and go to bed." Cassie said, "Yes I remember, I had been hearing noises outside during the night and I was afraid to sleep." "Well", Ben said, "do you remember what you said back to me at the front gate of the prison compound?" Cassandra gave a slight laugh, looked at Ben and said "Yes, I told you that if you would come home with me and tuck me in, I would sleep."

Ben began to kiss Cassandra's face. First on the forehead, then the nose, the cheeks, and then he looked right into her eyes and said, "That is exactly what you said. I told you then we would one day meet again and I would remind you of what you said, and tonight that is exactly what I'm going to do, I am going to tuck you into bed." And with that he put his lips to Cassandra's' and gave her a soft kiss.

Ben stood up, handed her the glass of wine, and told her to relax for a while, he would wait in the bedroom. She sat back in the bath, sipping on the wine, she closed her eyes and said a silent prayer of thanks, for she knew there had been a higher power with her tonight. Getting out of the bath, she knew Ben would be a gentleman, he would never try anything inappropriate with her, that he had already proven. He did not know of her trials with Dale, but he knew she was married, as was he, and he would only do the right thing.

Ben had come back into the bedroom and as he crossed in front of the bathroom door, he saw Cassandra brushing out her hair. He could not help but look. She was beautiful, and even wearing a gown, there was no denying she had an awesome body. But tonight, unlike in the weeks prior, she appeared frail. He knew the events of the evening had taken a toll on her. He would take no chance of doing anything to make her fearful or apprehensive of him. It was up to him to put her at ease and help her to feel safe.

As she had predicted, when she entered the bedroom, she saw Ben had pulled a quilt from the linen closet and put it on the chaise lounge. Cassie thanked him for the bath and the wine, but most especially for being there.

With that, Ben tucked her into bed and with a kiss on the forehead, she rolled over and fell asleep, she was emotionally exhausted. Ben crawled under the quilt on the chaise lounge.

The outcome could have turned out so differently, she could be dead, was all Ben could think as he watched her sleep. It was fortunate he had followed his instincts, had himself embedded into the prison so he could watch more closely the man he thought to be the killer. His research had proven him to be correct. The biggest hurdle was to get himself released so he could watch the suspect from both inside and outside of the prison walls. In his own meticulous way, he had noted the comings and goings of the certain prison officials, he knew he had to be right. With each killing, he narrowed his suspicions down until he felt sure he was right, even though the suspect's background and training didn't add up, it had to be the Captain. Ben finally began to drift off himself.

Around three in the morning, Cassandra awoke. Seeing Ben sleeping still on the chaise, she sat up in bed. She watched him sleep for a bit until he woke up and realized she was sitting up and watching him. He came over and sat beside her, putting his arms around her. After having a momentary break down and crying, Cassie looked at Ben and said, "Did we eat dinner, cause I am starving?" Ben started to laugh and said, "Let's go to the kitchen, I bet I can find us something to eat."

Sitting at the breakfast table, each enjoying a ham and cheese sandwich, they began to talk about how things had come about, and how Ben truly was from California. The Chief knew him from years before, and knew he had to have someone local law enforcement would not recognize. They created a history for him, making him a banker who had knowingly made some bad loans while receiving personal gain.

Once the Chief was aware there was a possibility the killer might wear a law enforcement uniform, he checked every type of law enforcement on the island. When it finally came down to checking out the officers at the prison, the only one with no real personal history made him question what the Captain might be hiding. He then spoke with Ben's Chief back in California and asked if he could recruit Ben as part of the local team for a few months. Fortunately the Chief in California was aware of the serial killings in Honolulu and the on-going search. He willingly allowed Ben to transfer over to help with the investigation. Once embedded in the prison, everything just kind of fell into place, even being made part of the team to work with her, it just fell into place, it was pure luck.

After a bit, they put away the food and returned to the bed-room. Ben looked outside to see the police unit still parked in the driveway. Cassie once again climbed into the big bed, but this time, Ben laid down with her. She under the covers, Ben on top of the covers. They both laughed, hugged each other, then fell back asleep till the morning light began to filter into the room.

Chapter 31

APTAIN LAW HID OUT in the heavy foliage for a while, then used his cell phone to call for a cab. He knew the police would be all over his Chevy Tahoe at the public parking lot. Wishing now he had not told Cassie his vehicle was parked there, but he never expected her to live long enough to tell anyone. Trying to clean the dirt off of himself and straightening his clothes, he waited for the cab and tried to figure out what to do.

He knew the first thing he had to do was get to his house, take a shower and clean up. His obsessive behavior could not handle him feeling dirty. Then finish packing up his gift and drop it at the Post Office as quickly as possible. The gift to his mother was something he had to get done, it meant everything to him. Not because he cared about sending her a gift, but rather he felt it would be the very last statement he would ever make to her. For him and his obsessive personality, it was like dotting an i or crossing a t in a sentence, it had to be done.

Getting home and rushing inside, he quickly packaged up the wooden box with the crystal necklace he had worked so hard to put together for his mother. It reminded him of the crystal necklace she often wore when he was a child and she would lean down to get in his face while she yelled at him. Her eyes were so green. Then her big crystal necklace would fall forward towards him. There were so many times he considered pulling it as hard as he could in hopes of choking her to death. Little Timothy had dreamed of holding her necklace so tightly her eyes would pop out while he choked her. He was only a child and he knew he could never hold onto her long enough to kill her, but he did think about it.

Now he was sending her his own version of her crystal necklace. If he had just gotten the green crystals, but now the four blue would have to do. Writing out the mailing label and taping everything up, he got into his truck and headed for the Post Office. He was about to achieve something he had only dreamed of and suddenly, he wished he would be there in person to watch her open the package. Oh well, just knowing what it would do to her was enough to put a smile on his face.

Once inside the Captain's house, the SWAT team members were at first surprised at what they found. They had entered the side of the duplex the Captain gave as his address on his driver's license. But they found no indicators he actually lived in this place. Detectives started to go in, too, but all of them were confused. Opening the refrigerator, they found bottled water and juice. A few snack items in the pantry, but no real food. Did he live here, they wondered?

Going in the master bedroom, they found a perfectly made bed, a couple of books and a television. One of the SWAT team looked in the closet of the master bedroom and found a few nice clothes hanging there, along with a robe. There were flip flops and slippers on the floor of the closet. Leaning down to look further under the hanging clothes the officer saw it. A doorway cut into the sheet rock where the two sides of the duplex came together.

Now they were all shook up! What if he was armed and on the other side waiting for them to make their discovery? They all quietly began to back out of the room. Best to get out of this side of the duplex till they know what's going on. With the right kind of weapon, the Captain could shoot through the walls and kill them all.

From the Post Office, Captain Law drove to a hamburger stand where he sometimes ate and ordered the biggest burger and fries on the menu. Once he finished eating, he drove back to his house. Police were all over his place, but by now he expected them to be there.

Once outside the officers heard the truck come wheeling up the street in front of the duplex. SWAT and the Detectives knew Captain Law had a second vehicle, a pickup truck, and here it was now, pulling up in front of the house with all of them standing there.

The Captain got out of the truck brandishing a high powered pistol. For whatever the reason police hesitated firing at him. It was as though the officers knew he would not fire at them. Despite the murders he had committed, in his own sick way, Captain Law believed in the brotherhood of law enforcement. Without warning, Captain Law put the muzzle of his pistol to his temple and fired. There was no doubt at that point, he was gone. Shocking to all who witnessed it, Captain Timothy Law had smiled as he shot himself, for in his mind, where his mother was concerned, he had finally gotten the last word.

After an officer confirmed to the SWAT members and the Detectives the Captain was indeed dead, they re-entered the duplex. In the closet of the master bedroom, the hanging clothes were moved to one end of the closet and away from the door. It was a short, custom made door, but the Captain could easily access either side of the duplex through this door. Passing through the door was unnerving for the SWAT member, but someone had to go first. They had no idea what to expect.

Coming through on the other side, the team member was again in a closet, in another master bedroom. Walking through this side of the duplex was like walking through a museum. Finding pictures, maps, notes, trinkets the Captain had collected with notes attached. The notes explained the significance of each item, such as purchased while watching the blue-eyed brunette at 1102 Black Pearl Lane. It was almost as though the Captain had set up a shopping list of where to get his next victim.

The map on the wall with pictures of women and their addresses was the focus for all the law enforcement gathered there now. There was no question the Captain was the deranged killer they had been hunting. It was agreed by all, he was probably the last person they would have suspected. There was just no outward reason for him to be on their radar. It was a lightning bolt moment for all of them.

On the kitchen table one of the detectives found an envelope. It was addressed to the police. The detective called the Chief, who was still with Cassandra, and with the Chief's permission, he carefully opened up the letter. Inside was a typewritten letter from Captain Law. The letter detailed how, when and where he killed each of his victims. Like his map on the wall, he was very precise in telling details of every killing. The Chief remained on the phone to hear what the letter said.

In reading through the letter, they realized it gave them one victim they were not aware of, it was Julie Genro, the woman who had gone missing. She too, worked at the prison, with Captain Law. When coworkers at the prison had notified the police of her failure to show at work, they informed the police she was always on the prowl for a "sugar daddy". In fact, they had waited a couple of days to even call the police, as no one had missed her. It was assumed she had found her "sugar daddy" and just left. Now the police knew she was dead and where her body could be found.

The Captain went on to write he was forced to kill her. She was a loser who kept trying to get close to him. He explained he had no need to kill her, but she had tried to use him and no one would use him, ever. More than that, she saw him watching Cassandra at the market. The Captain's final comment on Julie, she was no loss, the world was better off without bottom feeders like her, he had written.

The letter continued to explain the three killings outside the bar, the need for the fat butted woman's eyes. And how her friend happened upon him just as he finished removing her eyes. The friend was in the wrong place at the wrong time, but the world was better off without the three of them, too. The little man was an obnoxious drunk and hypocrite. His wife was, plain and simple, ignorant white trash. In his opinion, he wrote, they were all oxygen suckers, stealing from the rest of the human race.

The Captain also wrote he had no remorse for the four deaths of losers. The only murders he felt the slightest shame about were the two college girls. The Captain wrote he had even stayed with them a while after he had killed them, trying to explain why he had to kill them and giving them some comfort. He had even left each of them with a cold beer. His final comment was that even though the two girls were in college, they obviously lacked in common sense, they were followers, not leaders, to have trusted him because he wore a uniform and drove a nice truck.

When the Chief heard all of this, he could only shake his head. Once he found his voice he said, "And they walk among us."

Chapter 32

D ALE FLEW IN EARLY the next morning, he had been on the plane since the wee hours. Shane and Leigh were left with their aunt, Cassandra's sister, at their house. Dale was not sure what condition he would find Cassie in when he got there. He didn't want the kids to be frightened, or for Cassie to feel like she had to put on a front so the kids wouldn't be scared.

The Honolulu Chief had one of his unmarked units pick Dale up and drive him to the house where Cassie and Ben were waiting. Once there, and after meeting Ben, they all drove to the police station where Ben and Cassie read over and signed more paperwork for the charges against Captain Law. Ben, now feeling like Dale was there to take care of Cassie, said his good-byes and left for his hotel. Parting was much easier this time, Ben was not an inmate, but rather, a very close friend. Ben and Cassie knew they would have an opportunity to meet again. They left each other with few tears, but rather, a tremendous mutual respect.

Dale and Cassie returned to the house, took a nap, and later went out to dinner. Driving around the island afterwards, Dale made his apologies to Cassie, said he had been a fool, and she would come back to Texas to a different man. Cassie hugged his arm and said that was all she had ever wanted. They were going to make it as a couple, as a family, and once again, Cassie was smiling.

After two days of site seeing and resting with Dale, Cassie was starting to feel whole again. Initially she didn't know if she would ever be able to stop shaking. Dale had stayed close to her, didn't push anything, just relaxed with her. They ate dinner out one night, but Cassie suggested they get some groceries and stay close to the house and rest. Dale said that suited him fine. They ate on the patio most of the time, and once they ate at the wet bar in the game room while they watched the big screen. Together they walked the beach behind the house looking for more sea shells for the kids. It was fun for them to imagine what it would be like to live here forever, and in this style. Dale promised her they would return at a later date with the kids and have a real vacation. After all, now the kids have Hawaiian grandparents, Angie and Joseph. Cassie laughed knowing the kids had told Dale about their new friends.

When Tuesday rolled around, after sharing breakfast with Angie and Joseph and filling them in on all that had taken place with Captain Law, Cassie told Dale she was okay, she could handle herself. They both had a job to do, and the kids were missing them. Angie assured Dale they would keep an eye on Cassie, they would be there for her.

So, on the fifth day, a Wednesday, she drove Dale to the airport. Assuring him she would be okay, she said she would get this contract wrapped up within the next two weeks and come home. They sat together in the car and hugged for a long time, then Cassie drove Dale up to the entry of the airline. He got out, grabbed his piece of luggage from the back seat. He then leaned into the car and kissed Cassandra goodbye. With tears in his eyes, he turned and left. She watched him go inside the building and then pulled away. She wanted to burst out crying, but was determined she would not. She had decided this was the day she would return to the prison to work. She would not show up there appearing weak or incapable. "Pull yourself together girl, you've got a job to finish so you can go home.", she told herself.

Chapter 33

S ITTING IN THE PARKING LOT, trying to muster the courage to enter the prison, she recalled her mom telling her when she was eleven and her horse had thrown her, that you have to get back on your horse. You have to show him he didn't win, you are the boss. Well, now she was having to get back on the horse again, but this time it was herself she would have to convince she was the boss, or she would never go in the prison again. She laughed and thought to herself, it was easier getting back on the horse. At least then she could talk to him and ask why he felt the need to throw her off his back. There was no one but herself to talk to now, no one to scold, she needed to find the courage and move forward.

Walking in through the heavy doors of the prison, she felt herself cringe as the doors slammed shut behind her. The guards were all watching her as though she were an apparition. She held her head high and spoke to each of them as she passed. Finally one of the guards approached her and asked how she was doing. Cassie smiled and said she was coming around, still having a difficult time believing all that had happened, and that it was Captain Law. The guard shook her hand, apologized for all she had been through and said he was happy to see her again. She thanked him for his kind words, looked around at the other guards, and they began to applaud her. Cassie raised her hand, somewhat embarrassed and said thank you all, appreciate everyone of you. The first guard then escorted her to the utilities workroom where her teams were already working.

Kevin and Cotton had seen her out the window in the compound area with the guards and came to greet her at the doorway. Seeing the two of them, the look of worry for her on their faces, she kind of broke. Kevin put his arm around her and walked her on into the workroom. The other men stopped working and they all gathered in a circle. The guard remained in the room with them, for they all wanted to know what had actually happened. What was the real story behind Captain Law? During the days Cassandra was out, stories of every kind had swarmed through the prison. No one knew for sure what the truth was and they needed her to fill in the blanks for them.

Breaking it all down as quickly as she could, she told them what her experience had been and how she was in absolute shock when she realized Captain Law was the murderer, and he was there for her. Then of course they wanted to know if what they had heard about Ben Brock was true, was he really law enforcement?

Once the story was told, she decided to also tell them about the afternoon at the house when she heard the voice on the intercom. Apparently Captain Law had considered killing her then, but decided instead to test how long it would take for the police to respond to her emergency call. She went on to tell them what he said to her about "it not being his first rodeo, that he knew how long it would take for the police to get there, and she would be long gone before they arrived." Even as grown men, and knowing the Captain was dead, they were still creeped out.

Both teams were quiet, seemingly in disbelief. Cassie turned to see Lt. Applegris standing by the door listening to her. Cassandra nodded his way, for none of them had heard him come in the room. Applegris nodded back, said "Ma'am", and walked out. None of them could believe he had moved so quietly.

The next eight days both teams worked furiously to complete the job they had worked on for almost three months. Everyone knew Cassie wanted to return home, and they were all anxious to see their hard work in action, so finishing up became a real challenge to them. Cassie became more excited with each passing day, for each day she got closer to returning to Texas. She had spent her last Tuesday with Angie and Joseph, saying their goodbyes and exchanging addresses and phone numbers. She was truly going to miss them.

During those last days, Lt. Applegris stayed out of the utilities workroom, and stayed away from Cassandra. The men all noticed his absence, and so did she. As they were wrapping up the final day, Cassie walked down the hall to what had formerly been the Captain's office and found Applegris sitting there gazing out the window. Everything cold, stark and neatly in it's place. Still reflecting the Captain's obsessive personality. She lightly knocked on the door facing which seemed to startle him. Applegris told her to come on in, stood up, then he looked right at her and apologized. He apologized for his early behavior towards her, and the fact he worked next to Captain Law for eight years and never saw the demons in him. He said perhaps if he had been more observant of the Captain, his comings and goings, his lifestyle, everything, maybe he would have seen there were problems. Maybe six other people would still be alive and she would not have experienced all she had been put through.

Cassie smiled, and said, "If we all had a crystal ball, we would all be living different lives." Applegris smiled, looked down at the desk, and thanked her for being so brave and for not blaming him. Cassie said no one there was to blame for the actions of the Captain, for his problems had started long before he came to Hawaii. It was just unfortunate the ones who paid the price had nothing to do with his messed up way of thinking. Lt. Applegris agreed.

Cassie let him know they were about to finish up in the workroom and thought he might want to take a final walk through with her, the Prison Administrator and Warden. She said they hoped to be out of there by noon. Then, if he was ready, she and her team would need to be checked out of the prison. Applegris again stood up, said he had talked to the kitchen and the Warden, and had arranged a lunch in the staff dining hall for her and both teams. "Kind of a thank you and goodbye for all of you, to each other." he said. Cassie was momentarily stunned. Where was Lt. Applegris and what had they done with him, she laughed to herself. "Well thank you, Lieutenant. I think everyone who has worked on this project will appreciate a goodbye lunch. That sounds wonderful." Cassie said sincerely. With that they walked down to the workroom and did the final walk through and systems check with the Business Administrator and the Warden.

Chapter 34

THE OUTSIDE TEMPERATURES were down in the teens that winter morning. Sitting at her desk, drinking her second cup of coffee, she heard the door bell ring. She waited to let one of the house staff get the door, but on the third ring of the doorbell, she found she was the one rushing to get the door. Where in the hell is everyone? Bunch of lazy no good losers, why do I pay them for doing absolutely nothing! she thought to herself.

A delivery man stood outside her front door, bundled in warm clothes and hat, trying to fight off the cold. She opened the door, greeting the man with a curt "Yes", and he responded by handing her a clipboard to sign for the package he was holding. After signing, she took the package, nodded at the delivery man and practically closed the door in his face.

Once she got to the kitchen she found some scissors in a drawer to help her open the package, but first she stopped to read the label. It was appeared to be a gift from her son in Hawaii, but what could it be, it wasn't her birthday, Christmas had come and gone, and it certainly was not like him to send a gift for no reason. He wasn't thoughtful, and he certainly doesn't care about me, she angrily thought to herself.

She stood there for a moment considering how long it had even been since she had seen her son. She had divorced his father years before, and always felt like he would have preferred to live with his dad than her, but his dad let it be known he had a new family. Her son then went off to the academy, and always seemed to be uncomfortable being in the same room with her. Once he graduated from West Point, he left for warmer temperatures, New York was not his preference. And truly, that was fine with her, for they had never really enjoyed each other's company.

From her son's standpoint, it was true, once his dad divorced his mom for a younger woman, he could no longer bear to be alone with her. She had never been one of his favorite people, and now, as an adult, he could ignore her all he wanted. Perhaps if his dad had taken him with him, left her when he was a child, maybe even at that point of his life, things might have turned out differently. The decisions made by some that end up having a tremendous affect on others for years to come.

She snipped away the tape that was bound around the box, cursing under her breath the whole time. Just send the damn package without binding it up with five miles of damn tape, she thought. All this tape, just as dramatic as his personality, good Lord, grow up, she thought to herself as she cut the last strip of tape. Getting it open and pushing away the foam package peanuts, she was surprised to see a beautiful hand carved wooden jewelry box. "Well!" she said out loud, "maybe he has grown up."

Smiling still, she reached in and pulled out the pretty box and sat it on the counter. Somewhat anxious now, she opened up the jewelry box and saw there was a beautiful necklace inside. The necklace, with what appeared to be four lovely crystals of blue, so unusual, she had never seen stones like these, as she continued to stare at it, she pulled away the protective wrapping. As she looked more closely it hit her, these were not crystals! What looked like beautiful crystal stones were eyeballs, human eyeballs! She screamed as she backed away. The smell of formaldehyde was now wafting out of the jewelry box and taking her breath away. She was overcome with absolute horror!

Then she saw the card. Opening the card she saw her son's handwriting, like it was when he was a small child, in childlike block print were the words, "To my Mommy with love. I made this just for you. I HOPE IT CHOKES YOU!" It was then she could no longer take it, she leaned over the kitchen sink and threw up the coffee she had been drinking.

She was still holding onto the sinks edge when the housekeeper came running into the kitchen after hearing her scream. Then she dropped to the floor. For the housekeeper, seeing what was resting on the counter was enough of an explanation to anyone. The elderly woman crawled to the corner of the kitchen, huddled down, absolutely petrified, "What did he do, what is he thinking, what is he trying to do to me? What is he trying to do to me!!" she kept repeating to whoever would listen. And then, sitting in the floor, she peed herself, like a terrified child, much like the little boy she had abused all those years ago.

Had her son been there in person, for the first time in his life, he would have felt successful. For now his mother was feeling the incredible fear he always felt in her presence. He would have been pleased. Mission accomplished.

Chapter 35

As she stepped off of the planes walkway, she headed straight for the luggage area, loaded up her luggage and walked towards the gate to leave. Her eyes were immediately searching the people standing near the exit, looking for Dale and the kids, she could hardly contain her excitement at being home, back with the people she loved most. Then she heard Leigh and Shane almost simultaneously yell out "Mom!" She turned her head to the right and there they were, running towards her, with Dale pulling up the rear in a fast paced walk. Both kids threw themselves around her, Dale moved in and put his arms around her, hugging her close.

There was the loving comfort she had been missing for so long, it was there, it was back. She felt as though she was melting, then she opened her eyes to see others in the crowd smiling as they watched her family embrace, and for a fleeting moment was embarrassed. Then she caught sight of a shirt she recognized.

It was the pale blue Hilo Hattie shirt with the navy palm trees on it she had greeted Jay with when he visited her in Hawaii. She looked again and realized it was Jay. He had come to the airport to be sure, to be sure Dale came for her. He said he would never harm her relationship with Dale, but the moment Dale failed, he would be there to take her. She felt a surge of tears in her eyes as she locked in on him. Jay smiled, blew her a kiss, turned and walked away from the crowd. Dale felt her distraction and turned to see what she was looking at, but Jay had disappeared by then, only Cassie knew he had been there. She smiled to herself, for she knew without question, she was one of the luckiest women in the world, surrounded by people who loved and protected her. Life was good.

She kissed Dale on the lips, thanked him for being there, grabbed her kids one at a time and said "Let's make Dad take us all to dinner before we go home!" The kids hollered and Dale laughed, took her luggage and said, "Let's go, I'm hungry." Walking with a kid attached to each arm, she again smiled to herself and said a silent prayer, thanking the man above for seeing her through some of the greatest challenges of her life so far. She felt complete, ready to move forward, and more than that, she felt happy, for she knew she was truly blessed.

ACKNOWLEDGMENTS

To my husband, our son and his loving wife, our daughter, her kids Reagan and Logan and my mom, thank you for the continual encouragement to keep going and finish this book.

Thank you to my former boss and good friend, Marjorie, our daughter, Lindsay, and my good friend and neighbor, Theresa, for taking the time to read and proof for me so I could continue to write this story.

To our dog, Echo, for always being at my side while I write. Her love has no bounds.

All my love.

ABOUT THE AUTHOR

DIAN SCOTT grew up in north central Texas. Growing up in the rural countryside with only an older Sister to play with, she learned at an early age to use her imagination to create stories.

Dian met her husband of 42 years while working as a teenager in a family amusement park. Together they have two adult children and are the proud grandparents of two wonderful grandkids.

Now out of the workforce, and again living in the country, Dian has time to allow her imagination to run free and get back to doing what she enjoys, and that is storytelling. She is currently working on two more books and has two children's books ready for publishing. When not writing, she enjoys cooking for her family and walking with her dog, Echo.

A peaceful life, a close, loving family and the opportunity to write is all she has ever wanted, and she hopes her readers will enjoy the journey with her.

www.ingramcontent.com/pod-product-compliance
Lightning Source LLC
Chambersburg PA
CBHW072355190626
46811CB00019B/877